Grace's stomach lurched. She knew where this was heading. She scrubbed with the tea towel at an imaginary streak on the glass she dried. "I don't—"

"You do," Sean interrupted. "And you can't keep putting this off forever, Grace."

Not forever, no. But until she figured out what she was going to do about what sat upstairs in the bathroom drawer—

Sean plucked the tea towel and glass from her and set both aside on the counter. He tipped her chin up until she met the faint exasperation behind his gaze. "You know I want to marry you, and I'm pretty sure you still want to marry me. You said you wanted to wait until after the trial, and I did. But the kids need stability now. We all do. So can we *please* set a date? Or at least open discussions?"

Grace pulled back from his hand, dropped her chin, and stared at a button on his shirtfront, guilt and no small terror twisting in her belly. He was right. She *did* want to marry him, and they *should* set a date, but...

Sean sighed. "Let me guess. Not yet?"

ALWAYS AND FOREVER

An Ever After Romance

Linda Poitevin

Michem Publishing, Canada

Published by Michem Publishing, Canada

ALWAYS AND FOREVER

Cover art by Kanaxa
Interior design by Clara Stone

ISBN: 978-1-9894570-1-6

Grace Daniels turned at the sound of a key in the front door lock, one hand clinging to the stair rail, the other clutching the laundry basket against her side. Her heart wedged itself into the back of her throat. Was this it? Was it finally over? The edge of the laundry basket dug into her hip. Eight months of waiting...

The door swung open and Sean stepped into the foyer, his broad shoulders filling the doorway, a cane in one hand. Snug jeans hugged his hips and a white golf shirt accented the deep tan on his arms. Bottle-green eyes lifted to meet hers, halfway up the stairs. He wasted neither time nor words.

"Life," he said. "No parole."

Grace sat down with a muffled thump on the carpeted stairs. The laundry basket slipped from numb fingers, and she watched it tumble end over end onto the floor below, spilling freshly folded towels along the way. It didn't matter. Nothing mattered outside of Sean's words. Nothing outside of the sentence handed down today to the man who had murdered her sister—

his own wife—and then tried to kidnap his own children. To take them and—

Grace's brain shied sideways, refusing even now to go there. Refusing to think of what might have happened if she hadn't been able to stop Barry Walsh on that November day. Because that didn't matter anymore, either. Because the kids were safe now. Because they were all—

"You okay?" Sean's gruff voice asked, startling her with its nearness. He'd taken off his shoes and come to stand amid the spilled towels at the foot of the stairs.

Grace blinked, bringing him into focus. "I—" she broke off and shook her head. "I don't know."

Sean stretched out a hand and gave her knee a squeeze. "It's been a long road," he said. "It'll take a bit of time to process."

She nodded. "I suppose. I just hadn't expected to feel..." Sean waited while she searched for the right word. "Sad," she finished slowly. "I feel sad. This makes it all so real. I mean, it was real before, but..."

"But everything is more real now," he supplied. "More final. Julianne, the kids..."

She swallowed against the lump in her throat and blinked back a sheen of tears. "Yes."

"Ah, Grace." Sean set aside his cane, ascended to join her, and rested his good knee on the step just below her. He reached out to gather her into his arms, then kissed the top of her head and murmured into her hair, "I'm so sorry, sweetheart. *So* sorry."

Eyes closed, she rested her forehead against the strong,

familiar chest as she had so often in these past months, letting his warmth and strength envelope her, infuse her. He had kept her both anchored and afloat since that awful day. Kept them *all* anchored and afloat. She didn't know what they would have done without him. Didn't know how they would have survived. She still couldn't believe he'd stayed through it all. Stayed to love her, to love them all. And she wondered if he would remain when—

"Aunt Grace?" a voice came from above and behind her. She pulled back from Sean and turned to Josh, hovering at the top of the stairs, his eyes round behind his glasses and every line of his body rigid with anxiety. "Is everything all right? They didn't let Da—*him* out, did they?"

Grace shook her head wordlessly, a thousand emotions clogging her throat against the words of reassurance she wanted to speak. Sean gave her shoulders a squeeze.

"I'll take this," he said. He looked up the stairs. "Come on, Josh. Let's sit out in the back yard where we'll have a bit of privacy."

Grace wanted to object, to say that she should be the one to deliver the news to Josh that he'd never have to see his dad again. But even if she could have crowbarred the words past the lump, she didn't trust herself not to dissolve into a weeping puddle of relief that would end with Josh looking after her instead of the other way around. She nodded grateful acceptance to Sean and scooted aside for Josh, reaching out to catch hold of his hand as he passed.

"It's good," she managed to whisper huskily. "It's all good."

Relief clashed with profound sorrow in the boy's eyes, shining a harsh spotlight on the lie underlying Grace's words. Because, no, it wasn't good. There was nothing good about any of this. Josh pulled away and he and Sean headed down the hallway toward the kitchen and the sliding doors to the yard beyond, the boy slowing his pace to match that of the man who still walked with a cane.

Josh and his siblings had lost both parents now. There had been no miracle for them that brought their mother back to life or made it so that their father hadn't been her killer. And there was no good for the kids in the sentencing of Barry. No right in what they'd endured—or the lifetime of healing they faced.

Grace tightened her jaw and squared her shoulders. There was, however, safety in which to do that healing. Safety for all of them. Maybe that was enough for now. Maybe, without the pall of Barry's trial hovering over the house like the dark, suffocating shadow it had been for the last four months, they could finally move forward.

A faint call, muffled by a door, drifted down from the second floor. "Maamaaaa! I'm up!"

Despite the heaviness residing in her chest, Grace mustered a smile as she called back, "Coming, Annabelle!"

She heaved herself to her feet, gathered the scattered towels, and climbed the stairs toward the smallest of her responsibilities, her mouth tightening as she passed the bathroom and the possibility hidden in one of its drawers.

The smallest of her responsibilities *so far*.

"How did it go?" Grace pitched her voice low, so that the kids wouldn't hear from the nearby table where they worked on their homework after dinner. She'd been in the middle of making spaghetti sauce when Josh and Sean had come in from the backyard, and she hadn't had a chance yet to ask about Sean's conversation with her nephew.

Sean looked up from rinsing out the frying pan at the sink. "With Josh, you mean?" He glanced over at the kids, his mouth pulling tight for a second. "It went, I suppose. He didn't say much, but then again, what is there for him to say?" He sighed, and his gaze returned to Grace. "You're sure we can't get him to talk to a therapist?"

Grace's heart tightened in her chest. "If you think you'll have any more success with the idea, be my guest. He won't even discuss it with me."

Water slopped out of the sink as Sean gave the pan an extra ferocious scrub. "Freaking hell," he muttered. "What I wouldn't give for two minutes alone with that son of a bitch. The number he's done on these kids..."

Barry's presence loomed between them as it so often did, and Grace reached out to put a hand on Sean's tightly corded forearm. "The important thing is that he can't get at them anymore," she offered, but her words sounded feeble even to her. She tried again. "We'll figure it out. Let's just give him some time."

Sean flashed her an appraising look. "Just him, or you, too?"

Grace's stomach lurched. She knew where this was heading. She scrubbed with the tea towel at an imaginary streak on the glass she dried. "I don't—"

"You do," Sean interrupted. "And you can't keep putting this off forever, Grace."

Not forever, no. But until she figured out what she was going to do about—

Sean plucked the tea towel and glass from her and set both aside on the counter. He tipped her chin up until she met the faint exasperation behind his gaze. "You know I want to marry you, and I'm pretty sure you still want to marry me. You said you wanted to wait until after the trial, and I did. But the kids need stability now. We all do. So can we *please* set a date? Or at least open discussions?"

Grace pulled back from his hand, dropped her chin, and stared at a button on his shirtfront, guilt and no small terror twisting in her belly. He was right. She *did* want to marry him, and they *should* set a date, but...

Sean sighed. "Let me guess. Not yet?"

"I'm sorry," she whispered. "I just...I need..."

He wrapped his arms around her and pulled her close, his warm breath tickling the top of her head and his unending patience and understanding shafting like a knife through her heart. "No yet," he agreed. "But soon. Okay?"

The knife slid deeper. She had no response.

CHAPTER 2

"So? When's the wedding?"

Sean pulled back from under the hood of the minivan and regarded the man who had strolled up the driveway to join him. "Nice to see you, too, Gareth. And I'm fine, thanks. How are you?"

Gareth Connor, Hollywood heartthrob and the cousin who was more like a brother to Sean, waved away his words. "I have no time for small talk. I'm on my way to get the kids from tae kwon do."

"And you took a fifteen-kilometer detour?"

"Gwyn's idea. She's dying to know."

Sean cocked an eyebrow at his cousin. "And you didn't think to call instead of driving over?"

"I did suggest that, yes." Gareth shoved his hands into his front pockets and grimaced. "For the record, never try to reason with a pregnant woman who's a week overdue."

Sean held back a snort. Like that would ever happen in his life. He made a sympathetic noise instead. "Still no sign of the baby? She must be getting awfully fed up."

"She was doing jumping jacks when I left the house. We see the obstetrician again tomorrow."

"Good luck with that. And keep us posted."

"Of course. Which brings me back to my question. You said you wanted to wait until the trial was over, and Sack of Shit's sentence was handed down last week. So when's the wedding?"

Sean shot a glance toward the townhouse where Grace was watching a movie with the younger kids while he changed the oil in the vehicle. He'd poked his head into Josh's room with an invitation to join him, but the eleven-year-old had barely looked up from the book on calculus that he'd been devouring at his desk. Sean gave a mental shake of his head. Every preconceived notion he'd had about having kids had been turned on its head since he'd moved in with Grace and her brood. Josh was lightyears ahead of him in everything academic, eight-year-old Lilliane had turned out to be the most athletic of the four, and from what he could tell, three-year-old Annabelle showed the most mechanical aptitude of the bunch. As for six-year-old Sage...well, Sage he was still trying to figure out.

"Tick tock." Gareth's voice intruded on his thoughts. "I'm on a tight schedule, remember?"

Sean sighed. "And I don't know what to tell you. I tried raising the question again after dinner the night Walsh was sentenced, but she changed the subject and I..." He trailed off as Gareth stared at him. "What?"

Gareth stared some more. Sean looked down at the front of his t-shirt, then over both shoulders, then back at his cousin. He held his hands wide, bewildered.

"What?" he asked again. "Did I grow a second head or something?"

His cousin removed one hand from a pocket, pinched the bridge of his nose, and closed his eyes. "Please tell me you didn't propose to the woman over dirty dishes on one of the most traumatic days of her life."

The dishes had been clean by then, but Sean was pretty sure that wasn't what Gareth meant. He bristled slightly. "May I remind you that *you* proposed in a hallway full of people, with Nicholas wedged in between you and Gwyn?"

"Extenuating circumstances, and you know it." Gareth opened his eyes and dropped his hand to his side again. "For the love of God, Sean, the woman has been through hell and back, lost her sister, taken on four children—and you—and basically given up her entire life. I think she deserves a decent proposal, don't you?"

Well, when he put it that way…

"Shit," said Sean. "I'm a total ass, aren't I?"

"Yes. But a redeemable one. I hope."

Sean rubbed a grease-stained hand over his head. "Fine. You're the expert on romance, Mr. Hollywood. What do you suggest I do?"

"Do you have a ring?"

"Of course I have a ring."

"Then dinner out. Somewhere fancy. Tonight."

"Tonight! Isn't that a bit sudden?"

"Cold feet?"

"Of course not, but—"

"But nothing. You know the kids won't stay with anyone but me and Gwyn—"

True.

"—and if she goes into labor and has the baby," Gareth continued, "it could be weeks before we can manage four extras."

Also true. Sean rubbed his head again. "But don't I need to prepare a speech or something? And it's Friday —I'll never get a reservation at a decent place this late."

"You don't need a speech," Gareth said. "You need to tell her you love her and ask her to marry you. And let me worry about the reservation. Being famous has a few perks, remember? And now I need to get out of here before I get waylaid."

He jerked his chin in a direction beyond Sean's shoulder, and Sean glanced back to see a woman hustling down the street toward them, her platinum bob bouncing in time with her determined stride. Sean's mouth tightened. Adele Montgomery had to be the most annoying neighbor on the face of the planet, and not just where her complaints about the kids were concerned. The divorcee either had built-in radar where Gareth was concerned, or she was spending way too much time watching Sean and Grace's house in hopes the actor would turn up...and Sean strongly suspected the latter. He needed to get back into uniform soon, if only so he could stop by home with his police car on occasion. Maybe that would deter her intrusions. Or at least make them less frequent.

Sean turned back to speak to Gareth, but his cousin was already halfway to the car he'd parked curbside.

"I'll make a reservation for six-thirty," he called as he opened the driver's door. "We'll expect the kids at six. They can have dinner with us. That gives you" —he glanced at his watch— "just over an hour and a half, so you'd better get moving."

And then he was gone, leaving Sean to wipe sweaty palms against his pant legs and contemplate the breathtaking formality of the evening before him as he walked toward the house. Toward Grace. Toward his family. Holy hell, this was it. After a lifetime of denial and months of trying to convince Grace, he was going to get married.

Two doors down on the sidewalk, a sour-faced Adele Montgomery's steps faltered. Her accusing gaze met Sean's across the limited expanse of handkerchief-sized lawns. Sean gave her a cheerful smile, lifted a hand in a wave, and opened the door.

He was going to get married.

CHAPTER 3

Grace leaned both hands on the bathroom counter and stared at the little stick resting beside the sink. Slowly, she shook her head at it. No.

No, no, no, no, no.

A brick settled in her stomach, right beside where— her brain shied from finishing the thought. This could not be happening. There had to be a mistake. She picked up the stick and shook it. These things made mistakes, right? They couldn't always be accurate...

The result stayed the same: positive. Her gaze traveled over the six other sticks lined up on the counter. All, in varying formats and used over the past six days, gave the identical answer: positive. Her shoulders sagged. Seven out of seven. An entire weeks' worth of unvarying results. Even in her utter desperation edged with hysteria, she couldn't see much room for error in those odds. She raised her gaze to that of her reflection and stared at the shock mirrored there.

Five kids. *Five.* She could barely keep her head above water with the four she'd already taken in. How in hell was she going to manage *five*?

And how in hell was she going to tell Sean?

Her heart slammed against her ribcage at the idea. Sean. Sean, who'd never wanted a family in the first place, who'd already taken on her sister's four, who'd made it clear—crystal clear—that he had no interest in more. A declaration Grace had been fine with, because frankly, she'd had no interest, either. And now...now, there were seven positives laid out before her, and—

A rap sounded at the bathroom door and Grace jumped, dropping the pregnancy test into the sink with a clatter.

"Grace? You in there?" Sean asked. "I have a surprise for you."

She clapped a hand over her mouth to muffle the guffaw that tried to escape. *He* had a surprise? He had no freaking idea.

"Grace?"

She gulped for air, sent her reflection a stern look, and squared her shoulders. "I'll be out in a second," she called back. She scooped up the evidence and dropped the seven sticks into the back of her jumbled makeup drawer, then crushed the newest box and stuffed it into the bottom of the trash can with the others. She'd deal with later, after she'd figured out *how* to deal with it. Then, taking a deep, bracing breath, she opened the door.

Sean regarded her curiously. "Everything okay? You look a little flushed."

"Fine!" she squeaked. She cleared her throat. "Everything is fine. I just needed a couple of minutes to myself, is all."

Guilt flashed across his expression, and he stretched out a hand to brush the hair back from her cheek. "Damn," he muttered. "I guess I should've taken them to the museum today, after all. It just seemed like so much effort, getting everyone out the door, and you already looked tired. I thought the movie idea would be easier for you."

"And it was," Grace assured him. So the bags under her eyes weren't just her imagination? Wonderful. With an effort, she refrained from pulling away from his touch, a move that would only raise more questions. She forced a smile. "Seriously, I'm fine. You said you had a surprise?"

"Dinner," he announced, looking rather like one of the kids when they'd just presented her with a gift they'd made. "Out. Just the two of us."

"Out?" Grace echoed weakly, trying hard to admire the gift and not dwell on how she'd rather have a nap. "Out where?"

"Somewhere nice. For a little celebration of"—he waved an encompassing hand—"this. All of this. Us, the kids, surviving our first almost-a-year." He pulled her in for a hug and nibbled at her earlobe. "I think we've earned a celebration, don't you?"

Well, yes, but...Grace pushed aside the traitorous warmth triggered by his touch and thought about her bed again—purely for sleep purposes. Really. "Does it need to be tonight? I'm not sure I have anything clean..."

Sean abandoned his exploration of the sensitive skin along the side of her neck. "Gareth stopped by and offered to take the kids for us. With Gwyn due any day, it could be our last chance for a while. He said they'd feed them and everything. All we have to do is drop them off." He dropped a kiss on her forehead and limped down the hall toward their bedroom, adding over his shoulder, "I'll get dressed and then get everyone organized so you can get ready in peace. You have an hour."

Grace stared at the door that shut behind him, the objection she hadn't had the heart to make hovering on her lips. A muted, cheerful whistle drifted from their room, and the tinny tinkle of music from the kids' movie she'd abandoned rose from the family room below. She sighed. Maybe Sean was right. Maybe an evening out wouldn't be so bad. The kids would be thrilled to see Gwyn and Gareth's gang, and it would be nice for her and Sean to have some time to themselves, especially since it *wasn't* likely they'd have another opportunity for a while. Gwyn had been as big as a house when Grace had seen her a couple of days ago, and—

And dear lord, if those sticks were right, that would be her in seven or eight months' time, too.

Five kids.

Five.

With a last, weak glance at the bedroom door, she retreated into the bathroom to put on her makeup and stare again at the change in direction her life was about to take.

CHAPTER 4

Even in the chaos of their own four kids being greeted by Gwyn and Gareth's three, Grace couldn't help but notice Gwyn's narrowed gaze on her. As if she knew. Or suspected. Which was impossible. Wasn't it?

Just like all seven sticks are impossible, a dry little voice pointed out in her head.

Grace mentally told it where to go and dodged Gwyn's hug in pursuit of Annabelle, who hadn't yet removed her shoes. She carted the three-year-old back to the front entry and held her—shield-like between her and Gwyn—as she began unbuckling Annabelle's sandals with her free hand, trying to keep the muddied footwear off her dress. Trust Annabelle to find and wade through the only patch of mud in the entire yard before Grace had even closed the vehicle door.

She blinked as Gareth took the preschooler from her and set her on the hall bench.

"Let me do that," he said. "While I'm sure the muddy look is acceptable in some restaurants, *Au Coin du Foret* isn't one of them."

Grace blinked again. "*Au Coin du Foret?*" She

looked at Sean. "That's one of the hottest restaurants in the region. How on earth did you get a last-minute reservation there?"

"Not me. Him." Sean tipped his head toward his cousin. "Apparently being famous is good for something besides attracting the Adele Montgomerys of the world."

Grace winced. "Please tell me she didn't accost you again," she said to Gareth. "Honestly, in the six years I've lived in that neighborhood, she never once gave me so much as the time of day until she saw you visiting. Now I think she camps out in front of her living room window just waiting for you."

Sean snorted. "My thoughts exactly."

Gareth helped the unshod Annabelle down onto the floor, and she raced down the hallway to join the others who had already disappeared into the kitchen. "It's nothing," he brushed off their concern. "I've had lots of practice dodging her type, believe me. Now, get out of here before someone remembers they need something and you end up late."

He reached to open the front door, and Sean stepped out onto the porch. Before Grace could follow, however, Gwyn, silent until now, darted forward with surprising speed and agility to block her path.

"Wait!" she said. "I haven't had my hug yet."

"Um..." Grace said.

"And I need to ask you something," Gwyn added, her blue gaze steely. "About Sage."

"You do?" asked Gareth.

"I do. We'll be out in a minute."

Husband and wife exchanged a look Grace couldn't decipher, and then Gareth followed Sean outside and closed the door. Gwyn wasted no time in placing her hands on her hips.

"How long have you known?" she asked.

"I—" Tears prickled behind Grace's eyes, and she broke off to blink them back before admitting—because Gwyn's expression told her there was no point in denial, "A week, give or take. That's when I did the first test."

"How many did you do?"

"Including today, seven. They all gave the same result."

"I see." Gwyn said. "Does it help to know that I did three myself?"

Grace gave a watery giggle, then sagged against the wall. "Freaking hell, Gwyn, what am I going to do? I can barely manage four of them. How am I going to deal with *five*? And how in hell do I tell Sean?"

The woman who was rapidly becoming the best friend Grace had ever had offered her a wry smile. "Remember last Christmas, when I found out I was pregnant with Junior here?" She patted her belly.

Grace nodded.

"I'm going to share the same very wise words with you that were shared with me. Ready?"

Grace nodded again.

"Do you love him?"

She didn't hesitate. "With all my heart."

"And do you trust him?"

"Of course I do."

"Then just tell him. It'll be a shock, but he'll come around, and the two of you will figure things out. Together." Gwyn wrapped her in a warm, comforting hug, then set her away firmly and reached for the door knob. "Now take a deep breath and go have dinner with your man."

"Is everything okay?" One of Sean's hands found hers on her lap as the other steered the vehicle through the sun-dappled Gatineau Hills toward the restaurant. "You're awfully quiet."

Grace squeezed his fingers and made her voice light. "I'm just enjoying the scenery," she said. It wasn't a total lie, because while she may have been mulling over Gwyn's words, she'd always loved this drive. And she *would* tell him, but not tonight. Not when he'd gone to this much trouble to give them an evening away from all their responsibilities.

"It is beautiful, isn't it? We should bring the kids up for a hike this summer. There are a couple of easy trails that I should be able to manage okay with my leg. And camping. We should definitely take them camping. I'm pretty sure Gwyn and Gareth have all the necessary equipment, and I don't think they'll be using it much this year with the new baby. God, can you imagine being in a tent with that many kids *and* a newborn?" Sean shook his head with a chuckle. "Better them than us, that's all I can say. Ah. We're here."

Grace's stomach rolled, and bile rose into her throat as Sean turned into the restaurant's gravelled, lamp-lit parking lot. She closed her eyes and fought back the nausea and panic lancing through her. Sean would 'come around,' Gwyn had assured her, but with statements like that, Grace couldn't help but have her doubts.

Serious doubts.

Chapter 5

"A penny for them."

Startled out of her reverie, Grace looked up from pushing her *petit pois* around the elegant, gold-edged plate with her fork. Across the table, Sean leaned forward on his elbows, head tipped quizzically to one side. His green eyes reflected the light of the candle on the white linen tabletop between them.

"You're a million miles away," he said. "Was tonight a bad idea?"

"No!" Grace reached out and put a hand on his forearm, her fingers settling over tightened muscle beneath his suit jacket sleeve. "No, it was a lovely idea. I'm just...I was just..."

"Thinking about the kids and their dad?" he offered.

She seized on the lifeline. "Yes. It just seems so surreal, still, I think. That it's over, I mean. And that the kids are mine—"

"Ours."

"What?"

"The kids are *ours*," Sean corrected. "Yours *and* mine."

She looked down into the candle's flickering flame. "But they're not, are they? Or at least, they don't have to be."

The muscles beneath her fingertips flexed. "I'm not sure I follow."

Grace swallowed hard, searching for the right words. Words that would let Sean know he still had a choice in all this—a choice she needed him to make before he knew about the latest...complication. "I mean they're not your responsibility, Sean. Not if you don't want them to be."

A long silence followed her words, and then Sean's voice dropped to a growl. "Grace, what the hell is going on? You've been like a cat walking across hot bricks for the last week, and now you're telling me the kids aren't mine unless I—" His eyes narrowed. "Are you trying to call it off between us?"

"No! Of course not! Well...not exactly."

"Then what the hell?" He scowled. "*Exactly.*"

She bit her lip. "It's just...I just..." She stopped and drew a deep, steadying breath. Then she made her gaze lift to his. "Our relationship hasn't exactly gotten off to a normal start, has it? Between Barry finding us at the cottage, Julianne's funeral, and then the trial—not to mention learning how to parent four kids—and...well, things have been pretty intense, don't you think? And neither of us has had much time to catch our breath, let alone reconsider."

Sean's eyebrows stayed clamped together. "And are

you? Reconsidering, I mean?"

"No." The very thought made Grace's heart hurt. Her soul ache. She shook her head and repeated in a firmer voice, "No. But I need you to know that I'd understand if you were."

For a long moment—long enough for panic to begin fluttering in her belly—Sean said nothing, staring down at her hand resting on his arm. When he finally looked up again, his gaze smoldered with an expression that made her catch her breath.

Sean let out a long breath of his own and began speaking, his voice pitched low. "In the seven months that I've known you, Grace Daniels, you have been the epitome of your name. I have seen you take down a murderer, bury your sister, and step into the role of mother to her four children. You've changed diapers, kissed skinned knees, learned to cook, and been the anchor for a new family, all in spite of dealing with your own grief. So many moments I've looked at you and thought that I could never love you more than I did right then, right there...but you keep proving me wrong. And you just did so again."

Before Grace could fully absorb the words, let alone respond past the sudden, enormous lump in her throat, Sean pushed back his chair and stood. He came around the table to her side and took one of her hands in his.

"You'll have to help me get up again," he said.

"Wha—" Grace's question hung unfinished in the air as Sean lowered himself stiffly to one knee and she stared at him in astonishment. All around them, conversations drifted into silence as the curious eyes of the other patrons turned to watch the scene unfolding in their midst.

"Grace Daniels," he said, his voice husky and his gaze steady, "I love you with all my heart and soul, and I love your family—*our* family. I want to share your laughter and your tears. I want to be the shoulder you can lean on whenever you need it and the arms that hold you through good and bad. I want to raise *our* kids with you, I want to fall asleep looking at you every night, and I want to grow old and wrinkly and saggy at your side. I want, Grace Daniels, to be your partner. For life."

Speechless, Grace could do nothing but watch as he released her hand and withdrew a small box from his jacket pocket. He opened the box, and the deep, intense green light of an emerald blinked at her. Her favorite stone. He'd remembered. And he was asking—

"Marry me," he said. "Grow old with me. Laugh with me. Live with me. Love me as I love you, darling Grace, and please, *please* say you'll be my wife."

Her mouth flapped. She stared at the ring. Stared at Sean. Stared at the ring again. A distant part of her realized the entire restaurant held its collective breath, waiting for her response.

Answer him, you idiot! her inner voice ordered. *Tell him that you would love nothing better. Say yes, damn it!*

Grace raised her gaze to Sean's once more. She opened her mouth to speak.

"I'm pregnant," she said.

CHAPTER 6

Utter silence met Grace's words. Conversations still buzzed further off in the restaurant, where patrons weren't privy to the unfolding drama, but in the immediate vicinity, one could have heard the proverbial pin drop. Grace was pretty sure everyone around them held their breath.

She certainly held hers.

And held it.

And held it.

And—

Sean cleared his throat. "So," he said. "Is that a yes, then?"

The air left Grace's lungs in a whoosh. She stared at the man still on one knee before her, hope and elation tangling in her throat. "You're sure?" she whispered past the lump they formed.

"You heard the part about how much I love you, right?" A teasing light danced in his eyes, then his expression turned serious again. "I'm sure," he said. "I've never been more sure."

Powered by sheer relief, Grace launched herself

into Sean's arms, nearly knocking them both to the floor. Applause erupted around them, amid cries of "Congratulations!" in English and *"Felicitations!"* in French. But the noise faded into the background as Sean held her close.

"I'm sure, too," she whispered against the steady beat of his heart.

He buried his face in her hair, his breath warm against her neck. His chest rumbled with a chuckle. "Good. And now that we've established that and given all these people something to talk about for the rest of the evening, what say we skip dessert and go share the news?"

"The getting married news, or—the other?" She couldn't quite bring herself to say the word pregnant again quite so soon. This would take some getting used to.

"I'm up for both. You?"

"I would have liked to keep the" —nope, still couldn't say it— "other thing to ourselves for a while, but Gwyn already knows."

"You told her...?"

Before me? his drawn-out pause seemed to ask.

Grace gave a snort. "Are you kidding me? This is Gwyn we're talking about. She guessed."

He chuckled again. "I'm not surprised. That woman's deductive powers are downright scary."

"She says it comes with motherhoo—" Gwyn cut the word short. *Motherhood.* She drew back to stare at Sean with no small amount of panic. "I'm going to be a *mother.*"

He raised an eyebrow. "More than you already are with four kids in the family?"

Guilt held silent the part of Grace that wanted to tell him that she was afraid it wouldn't be the same thing. That this would be different. That she would feel an attachment to the unborn life in her belly that she didn't feel for the others. And that, somehow, they would know and—

"You okay?" Sean asked.

She gave herself a fierce mental shake, thrusting away the negative thoughts until she could examine them later. She'd just gotten engaged, for heaven's sake. To the father of her—oh, hell. There she went again. With more determination than finesse, she clambered to her feet and reached down to help Sean up.

"I'm fine," she lied. "And you're right. We should go tell the others."

Sean, however, didn't seem inclined to stand just yet, reaching instead for her left hand. "Aren't you forgetting something?" The ring Grace had all but forgotten about slid into place, its emerald light softly winking at her as another smattering of applause broke out at the nearby tables. "There," he said, with no small amount of satisfaction. "Now we're official."

Officially engaged. Officially pregnant. Officially terrified. Grace helped Sean stand and returned his kiss.

It didn't get much more official than that.

"It's about ruddy time," Gareth said once the squeals died down following the announcement made in the front hall. "And in case my dear cousin forgot to do so, Grace, I'd like to apologize on his behalf for taking so long."

Grace shifted a sleepy Annabelle from one hip to the other. The little girl nestled into the crook of her neck, her favorite stuffed giraffe—still sporting a cast made of Spiderman bandages from their time at the cottage—clutched in one chubby arm. Grace smiled over her niece's head at Gareth as the other kids retreated back down the hallway to the kitchen and the snack interrupted by Sean and Grace's arrival.

"Don't be too hard on him. It's not like he didn't ask before. It's just—"

"Just that he didn't ask properly," Gareth said. He shook his head at Sean, adding in a mutter, "I still can't believe you proposed over dirty dishes. Are you *sure* we're related?"

"Oh, leave the poor man alone." Gwyn gave him a

nudge in the ribs with her elbow. "The important thing is, he did ask, and she said yes."

"True," her husband agreed. "Which leads to the next important thing. When?"

Grace exchanged glances with her new fiancé. Sean raised an eyebrow. She shrugged. "I don't—"

"We haven't—" Sean began at the same time.

"Soon." Gwyn's voice overrode both theirs. She crossed her arms atop her belly bulge and looked pointedly at Grace. "*Very* soon."

Grace blushed. Sean coughed. Gareth raised an eyebrow. Silence descended on the front hall.

At last Gareth cleared his throat. "I get the distinct impression I'm missing something here," he said. "What gives?"

Sean looked askance at Grace. She hesitated for a moment, biting her bottom lip. Then she shrugged a surrender. Why not tell Gareth? Why not tell *everyone*? It wasn't like keeping it a secret would make it any less—

"Grace is pregnant," Sean said, with such pride underlining the announcement that Grace blinked at him. He grinned boyishly back and sidled over to slide an arm around her waist. He dropped a kiss on her forehead, his lips warm against her skin. "*We* are pregnant," he corrected.

Grace's heart swelled. Maybe this would be okay after all. It would take some adjustment, sure, but they already had four, and with Sean on board and by her side, what was one more? She stretched up to return his kiss, pressing her lips to his as Gwyn squealed and threw her arms around them both, group-hug style.

"I *knew* he'd be okay with it!" she exclaimed. She planted sound kisses on each of their cheeks, including Annabelle's, and gave them another squeeze, pulling them as close as her belly would allow. "I'm so *happy* for you!"

Behind her, Gareth started to laugh. And laugh, and laugh, and—

"Seriously?" Sean scowled at him. "That's your response to the news?"

Gareth laughed some more. "Don't get me wrong," he managed between guffaws, waving a dismissive hand at his cousin as his wife planted fists on hips and glared at him. "I'm thrilled for you. But after all the grief you've given me, and all the vows you've made over the years about no commitment and no kids, and now this?" He waved his hand again, encompassing Grace and Annabelle along with the back of the house where the rest of the kids had gone. "I'm entitled to a certain amount of amusement here, McKittrick."

"Your amusement sounds suspiciously like gloating," Gwyn said.

"That, too," he agreed. There wasn't so much as a hint of apology in his voice, but after a glance at his wife, he made a visible effort to control himself. Dancing dark eyes turned to Grace. "Congratulations," he said. "And I do mean that, Grace. From the bottom of my heart."

"Thank y--" she broke off at a movement in the hallway behind Gareth. Shifting her Annabelle load again, she leaned to the left, looking past him. Her gaze found Josh, standing at the kitchen entrance, near enough to have overheard their conversation. Flat, expressionless brown eyes stared back at her from behind wire-rimmed glasses, and in a heartbeat, she remembered the stories Julianne had told her about Barry's impatience whenever there had been a new addition to the family. His temper where the other kids were concerned. How Josh, as the oldest, had caught the brunt of that temper, especially after Annabelle had come.

How Josh would almost certainly remember all of that.

Grace's breath caught in her chest, tangling with the guilt already there. "Josh—" She reached out a hand toward her nephew, who radiated fear.

"Grace?" Sean murmured beside her. "What's wrong?"

Hands fisted at his sides, Josh turned on his heel and walked away.

The ride home was a silent one. Grace's terse explanation of Josh's behavior had been like a bucket of ice water dumped over the celebratory mood in Gwyn and Gareth's front hall, effectively ending the conversation.

The kids, sensing the change in atmosphere, had gathered up their things without objection. Gwyn had helped them pack toys into knapsacks while Gareth had tied Sage's shoes, and Josh had retreated to the van to wait for everyone. He hadn't spoken a word, then or since.

Sean glanced into the rearview mirror as he turned onto their street. In the deeply shadowed seat two rows back, he could only just make out the boy's hunched form crowded against the vehicle window. Sean gritted his teeth against the simmering anger that had settled into his core. His hands tightened on the steering wheel he wished was Barry Walsh's throat. The damage that man had done to those poor—

Grace shifted in the seat next to him. He reached over to twine his fingers with hers, welcoming the distraction.

"You okay?" he asked.

"We're never going to be rid of him, are we?" she whispered, her voice raw.

She didn't have to say Walsh's name. It already hung like a pall over their entire company—as it had to one degree or another every single day, if Sean was honest. A wave of helplessness swamped him. He squeezed her fingers. "We'll figure it out," he said. "Things will get better, Grace. I promise."

She nodded, but she didn't return the pressure of his squeeze. Sean withdrew his hand and signaled for the turn into their driveway. They unloaded the vehicle in the same silence in which they'd driven home. Lilliane took Sage by the hand and led her up the walkway to the house, Josh gathered up their knapsacks from the rear hatch, and Sean lifted a sleeping Annabelle from her car seat. Grace trailed after him, her face drawn tight with worry and fatigue. Josh didn't look at either of them when they reached the front porch, and the instant Sean unlocked the door, he pushed past him into the house and bolted down the hall toward the basement and his bedroom, not even pausing to remove his shoes.

Grace started after him, but Sean caught her arm and held her back. "No," he said. "Let me."

"Are you sure? He's—"

"Terrified," Sean answered. "I know. That's why it should be me, if you're okay with putting the girls to bed."

She hesitated, then nodded, accepting his words and the transfer of Annabelle to her arms. The lines of worry around her eyes didn't ease, however, and Sean stroked back her hair with gentle fingers. "We'll figure it out," he said again. "Together. I promise."

Tears welled in the dark chocolate eyes, and Sage sidled closer to her aunt, pressing against her hip. Sean's jaw clenched. It was a damn good thing Barry Walsh was in prison right now—for his own sake. He dropped a kiss on Grace's head and said briskly, "Right. Bedtime for everyone. We have a wedding to plan, remember? And if you two" —he ruffled Sage and Lilliane's hair— "are going to be flower girls, you're going to need your sleep so you have lots of energy. We can't have you falling over halfway through the ceremony now, can we?"

Lilliane's eyes grew round, and she looked to Grace for confirmation. "Really? We really really get to be flower girls?"

Grace shot Sean a look of pure gratitude, then

smiled down at her niece. "Of course. Who else would I trust to escort me down the aisle?"

Lilliane squealed and clapped, then she grabbed Sage's hands and began bouncing up and down. "Flower girls, flower girls," she chanted. "Sagey, we're going to be flower girls! At a real wedding!"

She stopped mid-bounce and turned to Sean. "We'll need dresses," she announced. "Long ones. Like princesses wear. Right, Sagey?"

Sage nodded solemn agreement, and Sean hid a grin. "I suppose you will. But shopping takes a lot of energy, too, you know. And to make energy, you need—"

Lilliane pulled her sister up the stairs with her, not waiting for him to finish. "Come on, Sage! We need to get to bed so we get lots of sleep. I'll race you!"

The thunder of feet faded down the upstairs hallway, and Sean looked down at Grace again. "Better?" he asked.

"Better," she agreed. "Thank you."

He stroked the cheek of the toddler still passed out on her shoulder. Annabelle, once sleeping, did not wake easily. "You okay to carry her up?"

"I'm fine. You're sure you're okay to talk to Josh?"

"Totally. I'll be up soon." Sean watched Grace begin the climb up the stairs, and when he was satisfied the child she carried wasn't too great a burden, he slipped off his shoes and followed in Josh's wake, making a mental note to talk to Grace again about moving. He knew she had all kinds of emotional attachments to the townhouse because of her sister, but as mature an eleven-year-old as Josh might be, he still shouldn't be sleeping alone in a basement. They needed more bedrooms, period. Four, assuming Sage and Lilliane continued to sha—

Sean's step hitched, and he nearly fell headfirst down the last two basement stairs. Wait. Make that five bedrooms, even if Sage and Lilli *did* share. Five, because the baby would need one, too. *His* baby. His and Grace's. Holy hell. He wasn't just going to get married, he was going to be a father. Stepping onto the laminate-covered basement floor, he looked at the closed door of Josh's room. A wry smile tugged at the corner of his mouth.

Correction: he was going to be a father *again*. Because damned if he didn't already think of himself as exactly that already. As cobbled-together as this family might be, it was *his* family, and somehow, sooner or later, he would exorcise Barry Walsh's ghost from it. For good.

"Josh?" He tapped at the boy's door. "It's me. Can I come in?"

CHAPTER 8

"Aunt Grace? Is Josh mad at you?" Lilliane emerged from the *Wonder Woman* t-shirt Grace had helped tug over her head and fixed her aunt with a solemn stare.

"No, sweetie. He's not angry. He's just...things are a little..." Grace looked down at her niece, uncertain how to proceed. As she was so much of the time when it came to this whole parenting gig. She heaved a sigh. Hell, who was she kidding? She wasn't just uncertain, she was completely out of her depth and floundering—every single minute of every day. She pulled her bottom lip between her teeth and gnawed at it. She had no idea how much to say, how little to say, or whether to say anything at all. Should she push the kids to talk about all that had happened in their young lives or just leave them to heal in their own way? Some days they seemed fine, coping and adjusting better than she'd ever hoped...and other days ended like this one, in a hot mess.

Lilliane pulled her pajama shirt on and returned to watching Grace. "Is it because he's afraid you won't want us anymore after you have the baby?"

The air wheezed from Grace's lungs. She gaped at her niece. "I—you—how—?"

Lilliane frowned. "You *will* still want us, won't you?"

The question, backed by just a hint of uncertainty, ripped Grace's heart from her chest and dropped her to her knees. She pulled the little girl into her arms and hugged her fiercely. "Of *course* I'll still want you. I will *always* want you, Lilli. Don't you ever doubt that, not even for a second, do you understand?"

"All of us?" a small voice asked against the side of her neck.

Grace squeezed her eyes closed and tightened her hold on the little body. "All of you," she affirmed. "Every single one. Because I love you. Okay?"

Lilli's head nodded against her. "Okay."

Grace pulled back a few inches. "And now I have to ask—how in the world did you know about the baby?"

"I saw the boxes in the shopping cart. You know. The test ones. I told Sage about them, too, but I said it was a secret. Mommy used one of them when she got pregnant with Annabelle." Lilli frowned again. "But she only needed one, and you had four. Does that mean you're having *four* babies?"

Grace almost choked. "Dear lord, I hope not! One is quite enough, I think."

"I think so, too. It's getting awfully crowded around here."

Out of the mouths of babes. Grace sighed. She

regarded her niece, one eyebrow raised. "You've been talking to Sean, haven't you?"

"Of course I talk to Sean. I see him every day." Lilli planted hands on hips and narrowed her eyes. "Are you going to get all forgetful like Mommy did when she had Annabelle in her tummy?"

"That's not what I—" Grace waved away her words. "Never mind. And yes, you're right. It is getting a bit crowded around here. How would you feel about moving to a bigger house?"

A new pair of small arms wrapped around her neck, and Grace glanced sideways to find Sage returned from brushing her teeth.

"Can it have a swing set like Nicky and Maggie have?" the younger girl whispered.

"Ooh!" Lilli clapped her hands. "And a playhouse! Can it have a playhouse?"

"We'll have to see..." Grace's heart twisted as both girls' faces dropped. "But I'm sure we can put them in if they're not already there," she added. "*If* I see two little girls tucked up into bed by the time I count to three. One...two...two and a half...two and three-quarters... two and seven-eighths..."

Giggling, Lilli and Sage leaped onto their respective beds and scrambled under the covers.

"Ready!" Sage cried.

"Three!" Grace exclaimed, climbing to her feet. "Just in time. You're *so* lucky."

She delivered the customary hug and kiss to Sage, then shuffled two feet sideways to Lilli's bed, stepping on a book as she did. Yup. It was definitely a bit crowded around here. She'd raise the idea of moving with Sean in the morning—not that she expected much in the way of resistance. He'd been trying to talk her into it for almost six months, but she hadn't been ready to take on another change. Or to leave the house where Julianne had—

"Aunt Grace?" Lilli was holding up her arms for her hug.

"Sorry, sweetie. I was just thinking about the new house idea." Grace blinked back the prickle of tears and leaned down to embrace her oldest niece, inhaling the soft smell of innocence. "Sweet dreams, darling girl. I love you."

"I love you, too." Lilli planted a damp kiss on her cheek, then settled back on the pillow. "Aunt Grace? Is Sean going to be angry when you have the baby? I think that's what's bothering Josh. I didn't tell him about the test boxes because I knew he'd worry about us. It's what big brothers do."

Agony shafted through Grace's core, knocking the support right out of her legs. She sagged onto the side of the bed. "Oh, Lilli," she whispered. She swallowed hard against equal parts pain and cold rage. No eight-year-old should have to think about things like this. If only Barry hadn't broken her arm at the cottage—if only she'd been able to put her full strength behind that kick and give him what he'd truly deserved for all the damage he'd—

"Aunt Grace?" Lilli's voice pulled her back again. Gently, Grace smoothed back her niece's hair and answered the question.

"Sean is going to be happy when the baby is born," she promised. "And he'll never, ever be angry the way your father was. Not ever. Understand?"

Lilli nodded, but she wasn't done yet. "Aunt Grace? Is it okay that I still miss Mommy sometimes?"

And the knives in her heart kept coming. Grace closed her eyes again, waiting out the new stab of pain. "It's more than okay, Lilli. It's perfectly normal. I miss her, too. Every day." She looked over at Sage, then down at Lilli again. "My bed?" she suggested. "Just until you fall asleep?"

Both girls nodded vigorously and threw back their covers. Together, they raced ahead of Grace, down the hallway toward the room she shared with Sean. She had no doubt in her mind that he'd be fine with finding them there when he came up. This had been the norm for the first few months of life together, when Julianne's death and the trauma of their father's actions had been fresh and raw in all their minds. Sage and Lilli between them in the king-sized bed, Josh frequently curled up on a nest of blankets at the foot. Sometimes Grace would return each to their rooms after a while, carrying her nieces and leading an almost sleepwalking Josh, and sometimes she would wake to Sean propped on one elbow, regarding her ruefully across the sleeping bodies.

Grace smiled at the memory as she followed in her nieces' tracks. And any man who'd stick around through all of that?

How could she have ever doubted him?

CHAPTER 9

Sean switched on the bedside lamp and then settled onto the foot of the twin mattress, careful to keep his distance from the thin, eleven-year-old body facing the wall. Even so, Josh curled up smaller, shrinking away from him. Sean's lips thinned. He cleared his throat. "So that was a lot of news to take in tonight."

Josh didn't reply.

Leaning forward, Sean rested elbows on knees and stared down at his linked fingers. "There's been a lot to take in for a while now, hasn't there?" he asked quietly. "A lot to deal with."

A tiny, choked sob reached him, and he squeezed his eyes shut. His hands tightened their grip on one another until his knuckles ached, and he wished with every particle of his being—again—that he could wrap them around Barry Walsh's neck instead. He forced his tone level. "Your Aunt Grace thinks you might be worried about how I'll behave with a new baby in the house. Is she right?"

For a moment, there was no response, then Josh gave a tiny nod against his pillow.

Sean swallowed against tightening in his throat. "I'm not like your dad, Josh. Just like Aunt Grace isn't like my mom." He allowed his words to settle between them, giving the boy time to absorb them.

Josh sniffled. "What does Aunt Grace have to do with your mom?" he asked finally.

"I never wanted to get married or have kids of my own because of how I grew up," Sean said. He chose his words with care, but he didn't hold back on his story. Josh was still young, yes, but he'd seen enough—lived enough—that he hadn't just earned the right not to be coddled, he needed not to be. "My parents divorced when I was three, and my mom wasn't good at being alone. She had boyfriends—a lot of boyfriends—and most of them lived with us at one time or another. Like you, I heard and saw things no child should ever have to hear or see. And for a long time—most of my life, to be honest—I thought all mothers were like her, and I swore I'd never have kids because I couldn't put them through what I had to deal with. Then I met your Aunt Grace."

"And she was different?"

"Very."

"So was my mom."

"I know."

"And so are you?"

"So am I."

Josh uncurled enough to look at him over his shoulder, his face streaked with tears behind the wire-framed glasses. "How do you know that?" he asked. "If you've never had kids and you never even wanted them, how can you be sure you won't be like...like him?"

"How can I be sure you won't be like him?" The real question hung unvoiced in the air, louder than the spoken one.

"I've been a police officer for eleven years, Josh, and I can count on one hand the number of times I've hit someone. And every single one of those times, the other person hit first—or tried to. I don't believe in violence as anything but a last resort." Although he'd certainly make an exception if he found himself alone with the man who'd put that look into a child's eyes. Sean pushed away the thought and worked to keep his voice even as he continued, "And I *never* believe in it where a child is concerned. Not ever, understand?"

"Not even if the baby cries and makes you angry? Or one of us does something to make you mad?"

"Not then, not ever." Sean regarded the boy steadily. "I'm not going to lie, Josh. There will be times when I'm angry with you, or when you're angry with me, or when Aunt Grace is mad at all of us. Families are messy that way. But we'll figure it out. We'll go for a walk to calm down, we'll talk, we'll listen, and we'll figure it out. And we will never, ever raise a hand to one another. You have my word on that."

For a long time, Josh lay without speaking, staring at him. Sean eased his leg into a more comfortable position, wincing at the dull ache that persisted more than nine months after the injury.

"Does it hurt?" Josh asked.

"The leg?" Sean shrugged. "Some days yes, others not so much. It's getting better. Slower than I'd like, but I guess some things can't be rushed." Such as gaining an abused child's trust, for instance. And rebuilding that child's confidence.

Josh nodded. "Sean?"

"Yes, kiddo?"

"Do you *want* the baby?"

"Very much," Sean replied. "As much as I want you and Lilliane and Sage and Annabelle. You're all my family now."

"Even if you didn't used to want a family?"

"Especially because of that, I think. Because sometimes, when we've never had something in our lives, we don't know how much we're missing it. You guys were what was missing from *my* life."

"Sean?"

"Still here."

"Are you sure my dad can't get out of prison?"

Sean took a second to remove the invisible knife from his gut. His voice was rough when he answered. "I'm sure," he said. "And even if he did, you have me and Aunt Grace to look after you, remember? And in case you haven't noticed, your Aunt Grace kicks butt."

Pride glinted in the eyes behind the wire framed glasses. "She does, doesn't she?" At long last, the boy rolled out of his curled-up-and-away position and onto his back. He tucked his hands beneath his head. "I can help out more, you know. So your leg doesn't hurt as much."

Given that Josh already did approximately ten times more than any eleven-year-old he had ever encountered, Sean had to catch back an automatic refusal. Getting Josh to be more of a kid would also take time.

"How would you like to start by helping me stand?" he asked. "I left my cane in the front hall, and I think I'm stuck."

Josh rolled off the bed and held out a hand, pulling him to his feet. Then he nearly knocked him back down again as he threw his arms around Sean's waist and buried his face against him. "I'm glad we're a family," he whispered.

Recovering his balance, Sean returned the hug and dropped a kiss on the boy's tousled hair. "Me too, kiddo," he said. He cleared the huskiness from his voice. "Me too." He put a finger under Josh's chin and tipped his head up. "Want to camp out in our room tonight?"

"Would that be okay?"

"Grab your pillow. I'll race you." Sean headed for the door and, smiling at the giggle that followed him, limped from the room.

CHAPTER 10

"Here." Gwyn set something on the counter and slid it toward Grace the next afternoon when she and Gareth brought the kids over for lunch and a wading pool party. "You weren't in the picture yet when Gareth and I got married, but our wedding planner" —she nodded at the business card between them— "was utterly amazing."

Laughing, Grace took a bottle of grape juice from the fridge. "Don't I get at least a couple of days to enjoy being engaged before I plunge into wedding plans?"

"You don't have a couple of days if you don't want to be waddling down the aisle." Gwyn sent a pointed look at Grace's waistline and the outline of the undone button beneath the t-shirt that fit a bit more snugly than it had only a week before. "Are you sure you have your dates right? You don't have twins running in your family, do you?"

Grace broke into a cold sweat at the very idea. "I'm sure I have the dates right, and bite your tongue, woman. Don't you dare jinx me with two!"

"Fine. But you're still showing fast and early, so you

don't have time to waste." Gwyn nudged the card closer.

Grace nudged it back. "Thanks, but we'll probably just do something small. A justice of the peace kind of thing, with dinner afterward."

Gwyn stared at her, one eyebrow raised, and Grace had to resist an urge to step back. While she'd seen Gwyn's "look" in action before, it was the first time she'd been on the receiving end it. No wonder it struck such instant cooperation into the hearts of Gwyn's children. Grace reached across the island for the tray of glasses she'd set out for the kids.

"You're kidding, right?" Gwyn asked. The question didn't invite an answer. Nor did she wait for one. "No. You don't just deserve a proper wedding, Grace, you *need* one. You all do." She jutted her chin toward the sliding glass doors that opened onto Grace and Sean's minuscule back yard, where Gareth, Sean, and the kids —all seven of them, not including the ones yet to be born—had gathered around to watch the water fill a newly installed inflatable kiddie pool.

"But a big wedding would be just more upheaval," Grace objected. "After all they've been through, the kids need stability. Calm. Heck, *I* need stability and calm. And believe me, I've seen enough weddings to know that they're the exact opposite of both those things."

"The kids" —Gwyn plunked herself onto a stool— "are kids. They need stability, yes, and you and Sean are already providing plenty of that. But they also need a distraction. Some excitement. Something positive."

"You're sure it's the kids who need a distraction?" Grace asked dryly. "It's not just you trying to take your mind off how overdue Junior is?"

Gwyn grimaced. "Maybe in part. I dreamed last night that I just kept getting bigger and bigger until my belly popped like a balloon and a whole herd of babies emerged." She shuddered. "It was not a pretty sight."

"I can imagine." Grace studied her cousin-in-law to be, noting the fine lines of fatigue around Gwyn's eyes and the faint tightening of her mouth. "But that's not everything, is it?"

Gwyn traced an invisible line with one fingernail on the countertop. For a long few seconds, she didn't speak, and then she said, "I had a letter from my sister yesterday."

Grace blinked. "I didn't even know you had a sister."

"And a brother. We're not close."

Grace bit back the obvious questions about where Gwyn's siblings were, and how old, and what they did, choosing instead to wait for Gwyn to continue.

Gwyn sighed, looking up to meet Grace's gaze. "She wants to come for a visit," she said. "I haven't heard from her since—well, in years—and now, out of the blue, she expects me to just forget what she—oh, hell." The words ended in a mutter, and she scowled.

Grace moved around the island and pulled up another stool beside her friend. "Why don't you start at the beginning?"

"Trying to avoid wedding plans?"

"Trying to avoid talking?"

"Maybe." Gwyn bit her lip. "Yes. It's not easy to admit that your sister is a self-centered—" She broke off, making a visible effort to gather herself. When she spoke again, her voice was firm. Detached. "Abigail is five years younger than me. She was always a bit of a wild child—I think my parents were worn out by the time she came along because my brother had been...a handful. They overlooked a lot of things with her that Grant and I could never have gotten away with. Too many things. What Abby wanted to do, Abby did, including marrying a man twenty years her senior when she was nineteen and moving to California." Gwyn's hand became a fist on the counter.

"I tried my best to stay in touch with her, and I thought we were doing okay. Even though we had nothing in common beyond our parentage, we called each other every few months, we wrote letters, we kept up to date on major events. She had a daughter a couple of years after marrying Dominic, and when I had Katie, I thought we finally shared something in common. A real bond. Because what's more bonding than motherhood, right?" She snorted. "Then Jack—my ex—up and left me alone with a three-year-old and newborn twins, and I asked her to come and help out for a few weeks. She refused."

"Oh, Gwyn...I'm so sorry." Grace put her hand over her friend's. "Did she say why?"

"No explanation. Just that it wasn't 'convenient'." Gwyn's blue eyes flashed with remembered betrayal. "We haven't spoken since. And then yesterday, the letter."

"What are you going to do?"

"Hell if I know." Gwyn scowled, then straightened on her stool and patted Grace's hand. "But enough about me. Back to the wedding idea, because yes, I need a distraction."

Grace looked over her shoulder at the backyard party going on outside. Josh dipped a hand into the pool and flicked water at Nicholas, who retaliated without hesitation. Her lips tugged upward as a full-blown water fight broke out, with everyone—including Gareth and Sean—scooping up handfuls of water and flinging them at random victims. Beside her, Gwyn cleared her throat.

"A wedding is a new beginning for them," she said gently. "For all of you. Think of it as a ceremony that marks the formal start of your family."

Grace watched the water fight morph into kids vs. dads. Shrieks and squeals filtered through the double-paned glass doors.

Dads.

Her heart smiled a little at the thought of Sean as a dad, and how naturally it had come. Then Gwyn's fingers closed over hers, and she looked again at the woman who was rapidly becoming like another sister to her. Julianne would have liked her. A lot. And she would have sided with her on the whole wedding idea, too. Grace tried one last time to duck the topic.

"It's just so much work," she said. "On top of four kids, summer vacation starting, finding a new house, this..." She pointed at her own belly. "How the heck do I find time to plan a wedding in all of that?"

Gwyn nudged the business card on the counter closer. "That's what Carol is for. And believe me, the woman is a whiz at it. And what new house? You're moving?"

Grace nodded. She picked up the business card and studied the simple elegance of gold print on a plain white background. *Carol Pal, Wedding Planner*. No fancy design or swirling, curlicue fonts. It was a good sign, but...she put the card down again. But.

"That's another reason we can't do a fancy wedding," she told Gwyn. "We talked about it this morning, and I've decided Sean is right. We're busting out at the seams in this place already, and once the baby comes..." She shrugged. "Weddings and houses are expensive. We can't do both."

"Actually..." Gwyn shifted her weight on the stool, looking both smug and excited at the same time. "You can absolutely do both—if we pay for the wedding."

Grace gaped at her. "What? But—no. No way, Gwyn. That's too much. We can't accept—"

"It's our wedding gift to you," Gwyn interrupted. "We talked it over last night, and we really want to do this for you. For you all."

Grace blinked back tears at the overwhelming generosity. To think that such good could follow on the heels of the horrors she and the kids had been through... but still. She shook her head. "It's incredibly generous of you both, but we really can't—"

"It's a wedding gift. You're not allowed to refuse. There are rules, you know."

"But—"

"Besides, you should never argue with a pregnant woman."

"You're making that up."

"The refusal part? Absolutely. The arguing with a pregnant woman part? Absolutely true. Just wait. You'll see." Gwyn slid off the stool and wrapped her arms around Grace. "You have been to hell and back in the last year, my friend, and you have lived up to your name at every turn. It's time to give yourself a break now. Time to let go of what you lost and celebrate what you still have. What you've gained. You and Sean and the kids—you're a *family*. You're getting married. You're having a baby. Those are all *so* worth celebrating, Grace. And we would love nothing more than to help. So please let us..."

Gwyn's voice trailed off, and she pulled back. An expression of bemusement settled over her features. Grace frowned.

"Gwyn? What is it?"

"Um...speaking of having a baby, my water just broke."

It took a second for the words to register, and then Grace yelped, "Now? You're having it *now*?"

"Soon, I think." Gwyn hissed out a breath, clinging with one hand to the countertop and pressing the other hand to the side of her belly. One instant, her face contorted with pain; the next, it eased into lines of utter calm. She grinned at Grace. "Very soon, if my history is anything to go by. And about damned time, too."

Sheer shock held Grace immobile. Then another spasm of pain pulled at Gwyn's face, and she leapt into action. "Gareth," she said. "I'll get Gareth. And Sean."

Leaving Gwyn holding onto the island and panting, she bolted for the sliding door and wrenched it open. At the last second, realizing her own panic would set off the same in the kids, she clenched her teeth in a semblance of a smile and forced a steadiness into her voice that most certainly did not exist in her body.

"Um...guys?" she called over the happy chaos. "Do you have a minute?"

CHAPTER 11

"Well. That didn't exactly go according to plan," Sean observed dryly, wiping his hands on the towel Grace had handed him.

Gareth, hovering over the paramedics and midwife checking Gwyn and their newborn daughter, who rested in the nest of blankets Grace had made for them on the living room floor, looked up at Sean's words.

"You think?" he muttered, appearing equal parts bemused and shell-shocked.

Gwyn reached out with her free hand to pat his ankle. "I did try to tell you I was quick about this."

Grace held back a snort. Quick didn't begin to describe the speed with which that baby had arrived. Forty-five minutes from start to finish, beating the midwife by ten minutes and the paramedics by fifteen. She could only hope her own delivery would be half so easy, rather than like her sister's thirty-plus hours of labor. She shuddered at the thought, then glanced up to meet the warmth of Sean's gaze as his arm slid around her waist. He ducked his head close to her ear.

"Are you thinking what I'm thinking?"

"That I'd kill for a delivery that fast?"

He grinned. "Well, about our own baby, anyway."

Gentle warmth suffused Grace, and she nodded. "Then yes. I'm thinking what you're thinking. I'm also thinking that you were absolutely amazing. How in the world did you stay so calm?"

The grin turned to a chuckle. "Remind me to tell you sometime about the twins I delivered in the back seat of an SUV in the middle of a snowstorm. For a woman who didn't speak English. Trust me, this was a walk in the park in comparison."

There was that word again. *Twins.* Grace's hand crept unbidden to the slight swell of her belly. She remembered Gwyn's observation about how early she was showing. Could she—she broke off the thought and made her hand return to her side. Of course she couldn't. She was just being paranoid. No, she and Sean would get married, move into a bigger house, and have a single, perfectly healthy addition to their already large enough family, and then raise that family together, doing their best not to wreak irreparable harm to anyone in the process.

"You're stressing again," Sean murmured.

"What?"

"You get a certain look of panic when you're thinking about the future."

"Do you blame me? Finding a new house, moving, planning a wedding, having a baby..." Grace swallowed hard, and her voice dropped to a whisper. Across the living room, the paramedics were packing up their equipment. "Five, Sean. We'll have *five* kids. How in hell will we manage everything?"

"I suspect we'll manage the way we've always managed," he responded equably. "One day at a time."

The panic didn't subside. "But—"

Sean's hand under her chin cut her off. He tipped her head back until she looked at him again. "Less than a year ago," he reminded her, "I was recovering from surgery for a gunshot wound that damned near killed me, and you were holed up in the woods with four kids on your own, hiding from their father while their mother was in a coma. Compared to that, an extra mouth, a move, and a wedding look pretty good from where I'm standing, don't you think?"

Well, when he put it that way...

He cleared his throat. "Speaking of wedding, Gwyn and Gareth—"

"Won't take no for an answer," interrupted his cousin as he joined them. "Especially after today."

Grace opened her mouth to object, but Gareth put both hands on her shoulders and scowled at her in a way that made her blink and snap her teeth together.

"Your fiancé has just delivered my daughter on the floor of your living room—which reminds me, I owe you a new area rug—and you are letting us stay the night in your bed while you take our kids and yours home to our place. Why are you doing all this for us? Because we're family, am I right?"

"Well, yes, but—"

"But nothing. You and Sean and the kids are family, too. And you deserve to celebrate the start of that family. And I will pay for that celebration. Am I clear?"

"Can we at least talk about it?" she asked, looking to Sean in appeal.

"No," said Gareth. "We can't."

"Give it up, Grace," Gwyn advised as the paramedics helped her up off the floor. Laughter underlined her voice. "You won't win."

Grace took a deep breath. She looked from Sean's shrug to Gareth's glower. She sighed. "In that case—"

"Good. Settled." Gareth released his hold on her and turned to Sean. "Thank you," he said simply.

Sean looped an arm around his neck and thumped him on the back. "All in the line of duty," he said. "But you're welcome. And now, let's get Gwyn cleaned up and settled so your kids can meet their new sister."

"You're sure you can manage?" Gwyn asked from the bed as Grace shooed the last of the kids from the room so they could get ready to leave and Gwyn could get some rest.

Grace winced at the thunder of seven pairs of feet descending the stairs to where Sean and Gareth had taken on the organization of their mass exodus. She glanced over her shoulder to find Gwyn, propped against the pillows, making the same face. Their gazes met and they both laughed.

"We'll manage," Grace said. "You just get some rest and enjoy that incredible little miracle you produced today." She crossed over to the bed and, with her fingertips, caressed the tiny, dark silken head nestled against Gwyn's chest. "She's gorgeous, by the way. Utterly gorgeous."

Gwyn smiled, pride and satisfaction radiating from her. She pressed a gentle kiss to her daughter's forehead and gave a happy sigh. "I've done this birthing thing twice before, and it still amazes me how instantly and completely you fall in love with them when they arrive." Her anxious gaze sought Grace's. "You're sure you're okay with us naming her Julianne? It won't be too weird for the kids? Or you? If you want to keep it for your own—"

"I'm positive," Grace interrupted. "There's no guarantee we'll have a girl, and it would be too close to home for the kids if we used the name. This is perfect. And the kids are thrilled to have her named after their mom."

Gwyn relaxed a little. "I'm so glad. I love the name, and I think she looks like a Julianne, don't you?"

If a heart could smile, Grace was fairly certain hers did. "She absolutely does," she said huskily. "And Juli would have been honored."

The newborn gave a wide yawn in response to being discussed, her face scrunching up. Grace laughed and leaned in to give Gwyn a hug. "And on that note, I'm going to leave you both to get some rest. You're sure you have everything you need?"

"I'm sure, thanks. Donna brought a starter kit with her, so we're good. If you decide to have a midwife for yours, you should give her a call. She's fantastic."

"I'll keep her in mind," Grace said, reaching for the

door knob and giving Gwyn an eyeroll over her shoulder. "*After* that wedding I'm apparently having."

"That wedding you're having *soon*," Gwyn corrected. "August is nice."

"August! But that's next month."

"And Carol is a miracle worker."

"You know you just had a baby, right? Do you think we can at least wait until tomorrow before we start planning?"

"Only if you promise to call Carol."

Laughing, Grace stepped into the hallway. "I'm going now, Gwyn."

"You can have it in our back yard. Carol said it would fit a hundred and forty."

Grace closed the door, calling, "Goodbye, Gwyn! Congratulations again! Sleep well!"

"But you need to apply for the license now," Gwyn's muffled voice filtered through the door, "because it takes twenty days in Quebec!"

Still grinning, Grace descended the stairs, accepted Gareth's hug, shook her head as she took the business card he held out to her, and continued out the door to join Sean and their small army.

CHAPTER 12

"Pink!"

"Yellow!"

"Purple!"

"Gween!"

Grace met the wedding planner's gaze over the heads of the cluster of little girls poring over the magazines and fabric samples she'd scattered across Gwyn's dining room table. It was their third round of trying to get a consensus on flower girl dresses, and the color choices remained firmly the same...or rather, firmly different. Katie wanted purple; Maggie, yellow; Lilliane, pink; and three-year-old Annabelle, "gween." Only quiet little Sage, sitting on Gareth's daughter Amy's lap, had refrained from offering an opinion so far.

Across the table, Gwyn rolled her eyes as she removed baby Julianne from her breast and tucked her against her shoulder. "I told you it was a mistake leaving it up to them," she said, patting her daughter's back. The week-old infant responded with an immediate, wet burp. Gwyn wiped her mouth with a corner of a cloth and continued talking without missing a beat. "You'll never get an agreement in a million years. And while I hate to point out the obvious, you only have a month."

"You may have to make an executive decision here," Carol agreed, studying the swatches the girls had chosen. "Or your wedding party may end up looking more like an Easter parade."

Grace looked down at the girls. They'd been practically bouncing off the walls ever since Carol had walked in the door. She so hated to take away any of their excitement. And she *had* promised they could choose...

"Aunt Grace?" Sage slipped off Amy's lap and leaned against Grace, who looped an arm around her niece's waist.

"Yes, sweetie?"

"Why are we called flower girls if we don't have flowered dresses?"

"Because we *carry* flowers, dummy," her sister informed her.

Grace shot her a warning look. "Lilli, we don't call people names."

Lilli, obviously trying hard to impress her older cousins-to-be, rolled her eyes, and Grace made a mental note to take her out for tea and a one-on-one discussion soon. It was a far more effective tactic, in her short mothering experience, than tearing down the little girl in front of others. In the meantime, Amy came to Sage's rescue, bless her heart.

"That's actually a good question, Sage, and it might

even solve our color problem." She reached out to pull one of the magazines closer, then flipped through its pages. "I know I saw it somewhere—ha! There. What about something like this?" She pointed at a little girl in the front row of a full-page bridal party spread. Blonde and cherubic, the child wore a knee-length, full-skirted, scallop-necked dress in a white fabric sprigged with flowers and leaves in all the required colors, cinched with a pink ribbon at the waist.

"They could each have the ribbon of their choice, maybe," Amy suggested. "And the guys could have matching ties."

And best yet, Grace could envision every single one of her own flower girls wearing something just like it. "It's perfect! What do you ladies think?"

"Hold on," Carol said over the babble of agreement. "I hate to burst your bubble, but something like that isn't going to be available off the rack, and a rush order for having them made will cost a fortune. I'm not even sure we could find someone to do it. Five dresses in a month is a lot."

Grace's heart fell, along with the faces of her flower girls. But before she could so much as muster a sigh, Gwyn said, "Do it."

"Gwyn, no. You and Gareth are already doing too—"

Gwyn cut her off. "When Gareth and I said we'd pay for the wedding, we figured on something way bigger than what you're having. Like three times the size. Believe me, there's plenty of room in the budget."

"But—"

"Are you really going to argue with a woman who's averaging three hours of sleep a night right now?" Gwyn cocked an eyebrow at her.

Grace glowered in return. "You do know that you use that excuse every time you want to win an argument these days, right?"

"That's because it works." Gwyn gave her a smug, complacent smile, then turned her attention back to Carol. "Find someone. Get the dresses made. I'll drive the girls over for fittings myself, if I have to."

Carol sent Grace a half-apologetic, half-questioning look, obviously uncomfortable at being caught between bride and paying client. "You're okay with that?"

With a sigh, Grace rolled her eyes and gave in. "Fine. But on one condition. I haven't had a chance to ask you yet, Gwyn, but I need a matron of honor. Would you...?"

Shocked blue eyes stared at her. "Me? You want me? But don't you have friends...?"

Grace thought back over the last seven months and how Gwyn and Gareth had been there for her and Sean at every turn, every bump in the road. Gwyn's quick wit and warmth had been a lifeline in a sea of change, and Grace had no idea how she would have managed without this woman who had rapidly become more sister than friend. But she didn't give voice to any of that now, suspecting that it would make the sleep-deprived, still hormonal Gwyn dissolve into tears. Instead, she met the blue gaze and said, "None as good as you."

Gwyn's eyes filled with tears anyway. She stood,

handed baby Julianne to an unprepared Carol, and came around the table to give Grace a fierce hug. "I'd be honored," she blubbered. "*So* honored." Then she pulled back with a watery scowl. "But I have a condition, too. You absolutely, positively can*not* call me a matron."

Laughing, Grace rose to give her another hug. "Deal."

"Now that we have that settled," said Carol, joining them to hand a squirming, fussing Julianne back to her mother, "can we please get back to the planning? You guys and your impossible timelines are killing me here. We still have a lot to look after. Cake, flowers, menu, music..."

She trailed off, diving into her oversized tote bag for another binder that she opened and set on the table.

With an inward sigh, Grace turned her attention back to the plans at hand, even as her brain added to the list that Carol had begun: *house, packing, move, baby...*

It was going to be an interesting few months.

More interesting months.

She made another mental note—a wry one, this time—to ask Gwyn if life ever settled down. Then the front door slammed open and Nicholas roared down the hallway and exploded into the kitchen to share his tux-hunting story, and she scrapped the idea. Because with this many kids involved, the answer was already obvious.

Still yammering excitedly, Nicholas clambered onto her lap, framed her face with his hands to be sure he had her full attention, and said, "And then you know what, Auntie Grace? When we got home, we saw them putting a for sale sign in front of the house next door, and now you and Uncle Sean and the new baby and everyone can live right beside us!"

"For the record," Sean reached out to clasp her hand as they headed toward the interprovincial bridge that would take them across the Ottawa River and home, "moving next door to Gwyn and Gareth was Nicholas's idea, not mine."

Grace slid him a sideways look. "But?"

"But what?" His focus remained on the road.

"But you like the idea."

"Not necessarily. Maybe. I don't know?" he hedged.

From the van's back seat came Lilliane's voice. "*I* like the idea. It would be fun living beside Katie and Nicholas and Maggie. We could go to school together, and play together, and have dinner together and *everything*."

Sean's fingers squeezed Grace's as he responded to Lilli. "There can be such a thing as too much togetherness, too," he said. "It's something your Aunt Grace and I need to think over carefully."

Grace pursed her lips. She'd been mulling over the idea since Nicholas had sprung it on her, and she still wasn't sure how she felt about it. But she hadn't ruled it out. "With other people, maybe," she murmured. "But I don't think it would be a problem with Gwyn and Gareth."

"What wouldn't?"

"Too much togetherness. Gwyn and Gareth are both very attuned to privacy issues."

"Well, yes, but—" He shot her a surprised look. "You'd seriously consider it?"

"I'm not sure. There are a lot of pros to the idea, don't you think?"

"Well, yes," Sean said again. "But there are cons, too."

"Such as?"

Silence met her question. It stretched for the entire length of the bridge, broken only by Annabelle's tuneless humming as she played with the finger puppets that Maggie had passed on to her. At last Sean cleared his throat and glanced into the rearview mirror. "Josh? Sage? How would you guys feel about the idea of living that close to Auntie Gwyn and Uncle Gareth?"

"I think it would be cool," Josh said.

"Would we still be able to have sleepovers?" Sage asked.

Lilli heaved a sigh. "Of course, silly!"

"Lilliane." Grace twisted in her seat to level a stern glare at her niece.

Her niece dropped chin to chest. "Sorry, Aunt Grace. That was another name, wasn't it?"

"Yes, it was. And yes, Sage, you would still be able

to have sleepovers. But we're not sure this will even work out, so let's not get our hopes up, okay?"

Sage nodded solemnly, but Lilliane wiggled a little dance in her seat and grabbed her brother's hand to high-five him. "We're moving! We're moving!" she squealed.

Grace opened her mouth to remind her that it was far from a done deal, but Sean shook his head. "Save your breath," he advised. "I'm afraid our Lilli is destined to go through life bouncing between absolute joy and utter despair until she figures out how to regulate her own expectations, and nothing you say will change that."

A surprised warmth unfurled in Grace's chest, first at the "our Lilli" part, and second, at his insight. While Grace, for reasons of leading by example, was careful not to use labels or names herself, the phrase *"drama queen"* had passed through her mind more than once in relation to her oldest niece. It was nice to know she wasn't the only one thinking along those lines.

The corner of her mouth tipped up, and she murmured in a voice just loud enough for Sean to hear, "Adolescence will be..."

"Interesting?" he supplied dryly.

She twisted in her seat and leaned her head against the headrest, studying him.

He raised an eyebrow. "Something I said?"

"No, it's just..." She shook her head slowly and pitched her voice low, so the kids wouldn't hear her words and all the reminders contained in them. "Do you realize that a year ago, we hadn't even met? And now here we are, discussing moving, getting married, joking about adolescence, and having a..." She trailed off.

He chuckled. "A baby," he said. "We're having a baby, Grace. You're going to have to say the word out loud sooner or later, you know."

She took a deep breath and moved his hand, spreading his fingers over her belly, covering them with her own. "A baby," she said. "Dear God, Sean McKittrick...we're having a *baby*."

"That we are, Grace Daniels. That we are." He gently pressed his hand against her, then turned it to thread his fingers with hers again. He lifted her hand to his lips, kissed her knuckles, and slanted her a grin. "Ain't no grass gonna grow under *our* feet, darling lady."

"Does that mean you're calling the realtor tomorrow?"

"I was thinking tonight."

"Of course you were."

"But we can wait to move until after the wedding."

"You're all heart."

"Not all," he disagreed. He returned their linked hands to her lap and dropping his voice in a way that made her breath hitch a little. "I do have other functional parts, too, you know."

Grace tried not to dissolve into a warm puddle on the spot. It wasn't easy. "That would explain the *we're having a baby* part."

"It would. Most satisfactorily, I hope."

"Well..."

Sean's fingers untangled from hers and slid upward along her thigh. His voice deepened. Softened. "Is that a challenge?" he inquired.

"Well…"

"Are you guys doing the sex thing?" Lilli asked from the back seat.

"Lilli!" Josh hissed.

Grace almost choked, and Sean pulled his hand back to grip the steering wheel, clamping the back of his other hand against his mouth to stifle his laughter. Ignoring Josh's admonitions to hush, Lilli continued.

"That's how babies happen, right? Katie told me. So if you do it again, does that mean you'll have *two* babies?"

Sean's shoulders shook and his face slowly turned purple. Grace sent him a withering glare. He refused to look her way.

"Wimp," she muttered.

His shoulders shook harder. Grace turned in her seat in time to see Lilli fend off Josh's hand as he tried to cover her mouth.

"Well?" her niece asked. "Will you?"

"That's not quite how it works, Lilli." With Sean all but collapsed in the seat beside her, Grace had no idea how she managed to keep her voice level. "But now isn't a very good time to talk about it, so how about we wait until we get home?" A thought occurred to her, and her mouth curved. "Sean will be happy to explain it to you while I get Annabelle ready for bed. Will that do?"

Lilli nodded agreement even as Sean gave a wheeze

of shock, his expression more than a little panicky as he finally met Grace's gaze. She smiled. He narrowed his eyes.

"*You*," he growled, "are going to pay for that."

Grace sat back in her seat again and dropped her voice to a murmur only Sean could hear. "With the sex thing?" she asked hopefully.

The van gave a wobble in response.

CHAPTER 14

"So that's it." Carol met Grace's gaze over the top of her clipboard. "We're done. You have a wedding happening a week from tomorrow."

"You're sure we haven't forgotten anything?" Grace lifted Annabelle down from the counter where she'd been washing the preschooler's hands and face after a spaghetti lunch. The little girl raced off to join her sisters and cousins in the backyard wading pool, and Grace dropped the washcloth into the sink. "I feel like we're forgetting something."

"Only our sanity." Sean's voice wafted out of the tiny walk-in pantry on the other side of the fridge. He poked his head out to roll his eyes. "Who in their right mind plans a move the week after they get married?"

Grace had no answer. Or at least, no answer suitable for voicing in front of their wedding planner—or the troop of kids tracking water and grass clippings across the kitchen floor as they poured back into the house. She held up a hand to halt their progress, reminding, "Feet!"

Then she sighed. Who was she kidding? With

boxes piled everywhere and the remains of last night's fast food dinner *and* their spaghetti lunch still on the table, she was worried about a bit of grass and water on the floor? She waved the kids in. "Never mind. I give up."

"Good call," Sean agreed. He opened the freezer door beside him. "Let me guess. Popsicles?"

"Yes please, Uncle Sean!" Unsurprisingly, Lilliane spoke for the group clustered behind her, but Grace was gratified to see that her niece waited until everyone else had their popsicles before she accepted her own. Their little chat with her about the responsibility that came with leadership had obviously had an impact. She placed a hand atop Lilli's head as the girl followed the others toward the back yard again, and Lilli paused to look up at her.

"Well done," Grace said.

Lilli beamed. "Thanks, Aunt Grace. I'm trying." She headed for the door, then hesitated in the opening, shooting a hesitant look toward Carol, who was packing her notebook into her bag on a tiny sliver of clean table. Relatively speaking. "Can I ask a question about the wedding?"

Carol stopped, giving the little girl her full attention and an indulgent smile. "Of course."

"Will it make us a real family like it did for Uncle Gareth and Aunt Gwyn?"

"I'm not sure I understand."

"Will we be allowed to say Mommy and Daddy instead of Aunt Grace and Uncle Sean if we want?"

Utter silence descended over the three adults in the

room, broken only by the high-pitched chatter drifting into the house from the rest of the kids in the back yard. Carol looked at Grace. Grace looked at Sean. Sean looked at Lilli. Carol cleared her throat.

"Well. I think that's my cue to leave and let you guys talk," she said, her voice husky. She swung the oversized bag over her shoulder and reached to give Grace's arm a light squeeze. "And to answer your question from before, we're not forgetting anything. I promise. Everything is in place, and I'll be at Gwyn and Gareth's next Saturday morning at eight sharp to get things rolling. All you have to do is show up and be your own beautiful self. Okay?"

Still bereft of a voice, Grace nodded. Impulsively, she leaned in to give the wedding planner a hug. "Thank you," she whispered. "For everything."

Carol returned her squeeze and gave her a quick kiss on the cheek. "My friend, you are *more* than welcome," she replied. She stepped back and gave Sean a wave, and a few seconds later, the soft closing of the front door marked her departure.

"Did I say something wrong?" Lilli asked, her brow crinkled in perplexity.

"Not at all," Sean assured her. He settled into a chair at the table and patted the seat of another in invitation. Lilli slid onto it and licked at the grape popsicle that had begun dripping onto her hand. "We were just a little surprised by the question, is all. How long have you been thinking about it?"

"Ever since you asked Aunt Grace to marry you. Katie said that when her mom married Uncle Gareth, it made them a real family so they could call him Daddy. She wasn't sure if it would work the same for us, though. Because Aunt Grace is...well, Aunt Grace."

Said Aunt Grace sagged against the kitchen counter, then took two steps to her left when she realized she stood on the exact spot where she'd found her sister, beaten unconscious and laying in her own blood. Her sister, whose children she now cared for. Her heart twisted in her chest. What the hell would Juli think if she could hear this conversation? Grace pressed the fingertips of one hand to her lips.

At the table, Sean nodded in solemn agreement with Lilli. "I can see where that could make things different," he said. "I suppose it comes down to how you and Josh and Sage feel about the idea. Is it something you'd like to do?"

Lilli studied her popsicle for a moment. "Josh isn't sure," she said at last. "But Sage and me..." She looked up, first at Sean, then at Grace. "They're not ever coming back, right?"

A breath Grace hadn't known she held hissed from her lungs. For the life of her, she couldn't respond. Didn't trust her voice enough to do so. Not around the tangled lump of sorrow burrowed into her throat.

Sean, bless his heart, rescued her yet again.

"Your mom and dad?" he clarified, and Lilli nodded. "No, Lilli. They're not."

"Then yes. We want to be a real family." Solemn brown eyes met Grace's. "Josh said he didn't think you'd want us to call you Mommy because it wouldn't feel right, so Sage and I decided we'd call you Mama instead. Like Annabelle does. Would that be all right?"

It was all Grace could do to nod, but that seemed to satisfy her niece, who smiled happily and slid off the chair. "I'll tell the others," she said. "Thank you, Uncle Sean! Thank you, Aunt Grace!"

Long silence followed her departure, with Grace and Sean both staring after her. Out on the lawn, six small bodies danced a dance of excitement as Josh looked on without visible reaction, his expression stoic, his popsicle forgotten in his grasp. Grace caught her bottom lip between her teeth. *Oh, Josh.*

"She's right, you know," Sean said quietly. He came to stand beside Grace, leaning against the counter, his shoulder warm against hers as they both stared at the yard beyond the glass doors. "We need to be a real family."

"I thought that's what we were."

"Apparently not in their eyes. And I'm not sure a wedding is enough."

Grace frowned. "What else is there?"

"I've been thinking about something for a while now. About maybe taking this family of ours to the next level." Sean looked sideways and down at her. "How do you feel about adopting them? Both of us. I know you're already their guardian, so it's not something you have to do legally, but it might be what we *need* to do, if that makes sense. Just to solidify things, especially for them." He nodded toward the backyard, where the girls had piled into the pool again, and Nicholas wavered halfway between them and his idol, Josh.

Grace blinked. "You would do that? Adopt them? Make them..."

"Officially mine? In a heartbeat, if you're willing."

She returned to watching the kids.

"Hey, Sean McKittrick," she said at last, in an echo of their first declaration a lifetime ago. "You know I love you, right?"

Sean chuckled beside her. "I suspected as much," he said. "But it's nice to know."

CHAPTER 15

Grace pulled her head out of the kitchen cupboard and groped for the cell phone ringing on the counter above her, cursing the interruption. She was already running way behind schedule—Gareth would be here to collect her any minute now, and she still needed to shower, but she was determined to get the last of the kitchen packed and—she glanced at the display and frowned at the name of her obstetrician. Calling on a Saturday? A flutter went through her belly. Sitting back on her heels, she jabbed with her thumb at the answer icon.

"Dr. Jeffries," she said. "Is everything okay?"

"Everything is fine, Grace," her obstetrician's voice soothed across the line. "And I know it's the weekend, but I thought you'd like to know that I found a little something unexpected when I went over your ultrasound from the other day."

"Unex—?" Grace couldn't finish the word. Her stomach hit the floor. Her rear end followed. She crossed her legs and pressed a protective hand to her belly.

"Not unexpected bad," Dr. Jeffries hastened to

assure her. "Just...well, there's really no easy way to say this, I suppose. Grace, you're having twins."

"I—no." Grace shook her head. She did a frantic, mental head count. That would be six children. *Six.* Plus two adults, it made a family of—no. Absolutely not. "There must be a mistake," she informed her obstetrician. "The technician didn't say anything about twins."

"It's an easy thing to miss at this stage. The babies are lying parallel to one another, and one is almost entirely behind the other. If you look at the picture the technician gave you, you'll see what looks like a shadow behind the one baby—that's the twin. I almost didn't see it myself, but I've had another colleague double-check it for me, and there's definitely two. Congratulations!"

Grace's gaze darted to the photo stuck to the fridge above her. "But...twins don't run in my family."

"They don't have to, especially if they're identical."

"Ident—" Another unfinished word. Grace closed her eyes. From down the hall came the sound of the doorbell, followed by the thunder of small feet and cries of "I'll get it!"

Lord, that would be Gareth, here to pick up her and the girls to take them to their house to get ready for the wedding. Grace raked a hand through her unwashed hair, remembering the shower she had yet to take. She made a monumental effort to pull her wits together.

"You're sure," she whispered. "You're absolutely sure."

"I'm positive."

An explosion of children burst into the kitchen, and small hands began tugging at her. "Aunt Grace, Aunt Grace! Uncle Gareth is here! It's time to get married!"

Allowing herself to be pulled to her feet, Grace mumbled a thank you of some sort to Dr. Jeffries—though she really wasn't feeling particularly grateful to the woman at the moment—and ended the call as Gareth followed the troops in. His keen gaze narrowed.

"Are you okay? You look pale."

"I'm fine." Grace managed a smile of sorts. "Wedding day jitters."

Gareth raised a dark eyebrow, looking unconvinced, but to her relief he didn't pursue the matter. Instead, he took charge of the entire procession for her, assigning fetch-and-carry tasks to the kids to make sure nothing was forgotten, and hustling Grace toward the doorway over her protests that she still needed a shower.

"I'm pretty sure we have water at our house," he told her, "and I am under strict orders from Gwyn to take you straight home, no delays."

"But—"

"Nope. No arguments." Gareth opened the van door and nudged her into the front seat. "You may be the bride but make no mistake about who's actually in charge of this affair."

"All right," Gwyn's muffled but determined voice reached through the voluminous folds of dress into which Grace struggled, "we're alone now. What's wrong?"

"Nothing is wrong." Grace poked her head through the neckline and plucked away the tissue covering her face for makeup protection. She held her arms high for Gwyn to tug the dress down and into place. Her about-to-be cousin-in-law crossed her arms instead and fixed her with a stare.

"I know you better than that, Grace Alexa Daniels. Spill."

Grace rolled her eyes. "Just because you learned my middle name from the wedding license doesn't mean you can treat me like one of your children."

"No, but you being family does," Gwyn retorted.

Grace's resolve to stay silent about the call from Dr. Jeffries crumbled under Gwyn's scowl. "Fine," she huffed. "If you must know, you jinxed me, Gwyn Connor."

Gwyn blinked. "I—what the heck did *I* do?"

"Twins. You gave me twins."

Her friend's mouth dropped open. She snapped it shut again and shook her head. "Oh, sweetie...no wonder you look shell-shocked. When did you find out?"

"Just before Gareth got to the house."

"So Sean...?"

Grace shook her head. "He doesn't know yet."

"Do you—does he—when—?"

"I don't know." Grace wiggled her hands over her head. "My arms are going numb. Do you mind?"

"Oh, lord. Of course!" Gwyn sprang forward and

tugged the snug-fitting dress into place and then zipped it up, struggling with where the fabric strained across Grace's belly, even though the final fitting had been less than a week ago. She lifted her gaze to Grace's.

Grace felt her face crumple. "Dear God, Gwyn. *Twins?*"

"Hush! No tears!" Gwyn shoved a fresh tissue into her hand and flapped her hands, fan-like, in front of Grace's nose. "You'll ruin your makeup, and we don't have time to redo it. The ceremony starts in fifteen minutes."

"But *twins*. What in hell am I supposed to do with *two* babies?"

"Be grateful they're not triplets?"

Grace snort-laughed through the threatening tears of panic. "Be serious."

"I am. That's how I got through many times with Maggie and Nicholas, believe me."

"But you already knew how to be a mother. You had Katie, and—"

"I don't know whether to hug you or smack you upside the head sometimes, Grace Daniels." Gwyn moved in to wrap her arms around Grace, touching her forehead to hers. "What do you think you've been doing for the last eight months, you silly nit? Playing house? You're every inch as much a mother as I am, and anyone who wants to argue that can answer to me. You included." She tightened her hold and rested her chin on Grace's shoulder, rocking her back and forth. "You are the most amazing woman I've ever met, bar none, and you and Sean are wonderful parents. You will raise two babies the same way you would have raised one, by making mistakes and being messy and loving them with all your hearts just the way you do the others. Are we clear?"

Grace heaved a shuddering sigh and dabbed at her eyes with the crumpled tissue. "Thank you," she whispered, drawing back far enough to kiss Gwyn's cheek. "I don't know how I'd manage without you."

Gwyn blinked back tears of her own and returned the cheek peck. "You'll never have to find out because you'll be living next door," she said briskly. "And if that isn't serendipity, I don't know what is."

Grace smiled as they stepped back from their hug. "Agreed."

"And now" —Gwyn picked up the circle of flowers that was Grace's headpiece— "it's time to quit dithering and get you married."

Grace obediently bent her knees so Gwyn could reach her head. "What about Sean? When do I tell him?"

"No idea, but *please* let me be there to see his face when you do?"

"Gwynneth Connor, you can be truly awful sometimes," Grace accused, but her giggle took the sting from her words, and Gwyn gave her a wicked grin in return.

"I really can be, can't I?" She secured the flower crown in place, gave Grace's hair a final pat, and stepped back. Her expression softened and her eyes shimmered. "Oh, sweetie...you look *so* beautiful!"

She placed her hands on Grace's shoulders and

turned her to face the full-length mirror on the back of the bedroom door. Grace's breath hitched as she stared at her reflection. From the neckline that plunged between her breasts to meet a beaded appliqué, to the cascade of satin that fell from there to the floor around her ankles, the sleeveless white gown was simplicity itself. And it was perfect. As was the crown of tiny flowers that matched her bouquet, in all the colors the girls had wanted.

Gentle fingers swept her long, dark hair over her shoulders to rest against her back. "Beautiful," Gwyn said again. "Now...are you ready to get married?"

"I am," Grace responded, her heart swelling with sheer joy. Oblivious to dress, crown, and hair alike, she whipped around and gave her matron—no, *maid*—of honor a hug that squeezed the air from Gwyn's lungs in a whoosh. "I really am."

CHAPTER 16

"Sean?" Josh's quiet voice cut across the strains of Pachelbel's *Canon in D* that drifted in through the open French doors leading into Gwyn and Gareth's back yard. Sean glanced up from pinning the pink rose boutonniere to the lapel of the boy's gray suit. Serious brown eyes regarded him from behind the wire-framed glasses.

He raised an eyebrow. "What is it, kiddo?"

"I've been thinking about what you asked last week. The adoption thing. Would it still be okay for me to say yes?"

If there was one thing Sean had learned about kids over the last eight months, it was that they never picked an opportune time to raise difficult subjects. Ever. He swallowed and blinked back the sheen that overlaid the world. If Grace found him standing at the altar looking like this, they'd both break down in tears. What a wedding *that* would be.

On the other hand, he wasn't about to put off Josh's question, either. He cleared his throat. "Is that what you want?"

"I think so." Josh hesitated, looking as if he might say more. Sean waited. "I can still remember my mom, right? And it's okay to still love her?"

Sean blinked faster and tried not to choke. Freaking hell, these kids and their innocence were going to be the death of him. After all they'd been through, all they'd seen and survived...

He cleared his throat a second time. Pachelbel rose in volume, Carol's not-so-subtle cue to them to take their places at the entrance to the massive outdoor tent that ate up most of the backyard. Gareth emerged from the tent and started toward the house. His gaze met Sean's, questioning, and then his step hitched as Sean shook his head very slightly. He nodded, turned on his heel, and caught hold of Nicholas's shoulder as his stepson tried to dodge around him. The two of them disappeared into the tent again. Sean turned back to Josh.

"It's more than okay to still love your mom, Josh. Your Aunt Grace and I *want* you to keep loving her. She's a part of you and your sisters, and we don't ever want you to forget that. Or her. You can talk about her as much as you want, and you can ask your aunt questions about her anytime. Okay?"

"But my dad is part of us, too." The eyes behind the glasses clouded over, and the boy's jaw tightened. "Do I still have to love him after what he did?"

Yup. They'd definitely be the death of him.

"Not if you don't want to," Sean replied carefully. "But it's okay if you do."

"I'd rather love you. As my dad, I mean. If that's all right."

Someone *ahemmed* discreetly behind Sean, and he turned to find Gwyn poking her head into the room, one eyebrow raised. Her gaze darted between him and Josh. "Everything okay?" she whispered. "We're ready when you are."

"I'm sorry," Josh said. "I should have waited. We can talk later."

No way was Sean waiting to finish this. "Give us five?" he asked Gwyn.

"Of course." She withdrew again, and Sean turned back to Josh.

"I would be honored," he answered Josh's last question. "And so would your Aunt Grace."

"It might take me a while to remember not to call her Aunt Grace anymore. Or you Sean."

"I imagine it will take us a while, too. Big changes are like that, and this is a pretty big change."

Josh nodded. "How will it work? Will we have to go to court the way we did to talk about Da—him?"

"It will be a different court, with a different judge. Smaller. The court, I mean, not the judge."

Josh smiled.

"Luc—he's the man your Aunt Grace borrowed the cottage from—is a family lawyer, and he'll do all the paperwork for us," Sean continued. "The judge might want to talk to you, to make sure this is what you want, but it won't be scary like it was when you had to talk about Barry."

"Barry." A thoughtful expression crossed Josh's face. "I think I'd like to call him that, too."

"I think that would be fine."

"And do I have to wait until after the adoption before I can call you Dad?"

Aaaand there was the lump again.

Sean coughed. "Not if you don't want to."

"Well then, *Dad*," Josh grinned at the word, "don't you think it's time you and *Mom* got married?"

"I do," said Sean, pulling him in for a fierce hug and dropping a kiss on top of the tousled head. "I definitely do."

Sean grasped Grace's free hand as she, Lilliane, Sage, and Annabelle stopped beside him and Josh just outside the tent's entrance. He lifted it and brushed his lips across her knuckles, sending a jolt of electricity through her. "You," he said huskily, "look stunning."

Grace blushed. "You clean up pretty good yourself."

"Three nights," he muttered, leaning in so only she could hear. "Three nights of just the two of us. Do you have any idea of how much I'm looking forward to that?"

"Probably about as much as I am," she said, her heart giving a happy flutter at the thought. She dropped her voice to a whisper. "Gwyn said there was a problem with Josh?"

"It's all sorted out. I'll tell you about it later." He tucked her fingers through the crook of his arm.

"Gareth said he thought there was a problem with you when he picked you up?"

Her heart fluttered again. Her belly followed suit. "I'll tell you about it later."

She thought he might object, but he nodded agreement instead. "Probably best, given that we've already kept everyone waiting. You ready?"

Grace considered the scope of the words. Ready to be married. Ready to move to a new home. Ready to have not one but two babies. Ready to be a family. It was an awful lot to be ready for, but as she looked at the cluster of bright, hopeful faces surrounding them, she felt exactly that. Because with Sean at her side, she was ready for it all. She smiled.

"More than," she said.

And then she and Sean led their little procession—their family—down the aisle to where Gwyn and Gareth waited for them with Katie, Maggie, Nicholas, and Amy.

CHAPTER 17

Grace snuggled against Sean's shoulder, wrapped in his arms and a contentment both fierce and peaceful as they swayed to the music drifting through the tent. Tables and chairs had been moved to the perimeter, the red carpet rolled up from the dance floor laid down by the event company, and a DJ installed on the stage that had been the podium for their vows.

Their wedding vows.

Because after the nine short months into which they'd already crammed a lifetime, they'd finally done it. They were married. Husband and wife. An official family. Which reminded her...

She tipped her head back to look up at Sean. "Do I get the Josh story now?"

Her husband—*husband*—smiled back. "He wants to go through with the adoption." His arm tightened around her waist as she missed a step and stumbled.

"Really? He's sure?"

Sean nodded. "And he wants to call his dad 'Barry'."

"Does that mean...?"

Sean nodded, his grin nearly splitting his face. "I've become Dad."

"And—and me?"

"You're Mom if you want to be."

Grace thought about it for a long few seconds, wondering what her sister would have said if she were here. Deciding that Juli would want the kids to move on. Vowing to keep her memory alive for them in every other way that she could. Still struggling with the idea. "It will take some getting used to."

Sean chuckled. "That's what Josh said. But I think we can figure it out."

They danced on, limited by Sean's recovering leg but both unfazed by it. Ten thousand fairy lights twinkled across the tent's roof, each carefully positioned under the watchful eye of their planner, Carol, who had left no detail unsupervised. Laughter wove itself through the old Luther Vandross song, *Always and Forever*, underscoring the mellow, gentle voice that sang of love. Grace glanced toward the source of hilarity and saw Gareth's father, Steffan, pulling a coin from behind Annabelle's ear as she sat on his wife Alwen's knee. Noticing her gaze, Alwen gave her a broad smile and blew a kiss her way. Grace waved back.

"Gareth's parents are amazing," she said to Sean. "Coming all the way over from Wales for the wedding and taking in our brood like their own. I hope he knows how lucky he is to have them."

"He knows. So do I. They've always been that way about family." Sean hitched her closer, his hand drifting down from her back to rest on her hip. "Your turn.

What were you so upset about when Gareth went to pick you up? And while you're explaining things, maybe you can tell me what you were doing packing the kitchen in the first place. On our wedding day. Really?"

"It was the last cupboard, and I just wanted it done. You do realize we move three days after we get back from Prince Edward County, right?" Grace waved off his objection and rolling eyes. "And I wasn't upset, exactly...more like shocked."

"By...?"

"Dr. Jeffries called."

"The obstetrician?" Sean pulled back, his brow furrowed. "Is everything okay?"

"Everything is fine." Grace bit her lip, bracing for the announcement she needed to make. Cringing from it. "It's just...a little bit finer than we anticipated."

Sean's frown deepened. "I'm not following."

She took a deep breath, and because she'd decided there was no best way to drop this particular bombshell, said, "Twins, Sean. We're having twins."

Her new husband stopped dead in his tracks, paled, and gaped at her. "We're *what*?"

"You're sure you're okay to travel tomorrow? You're not too tired? We can just stay at a hotel here in town, or even at the hou—"

Grace reached up to place a finger across Sean's lips, stopping him mid-word. She scowled. "Sean

McKittrick, are you trying to renege on our honeymoon?"

"Of course not—I just..." Sean's gaze shifted to Gwyn in search of support. She shrugged, swaying gently in place with baby Julianne cradled against one shoulder.

"Don't look at me," she said. "I was waterskiing the week before I gave birth to Nicholas and Maggie."

"Not helping, Gwyn," Sean growled.

"Not trying to, Sean." Gwyn patted his cheek. "She's pregnant, not an invalid. She's fine, the babies are fine, everyone is fine. Now for heaven's sake, go and take advantage of your three childless days and nights with your new wife, would you? You have no idea how rare that kind of peace is going to be in your future."

"Or how grumpy I'll be if I don't get those three days and nights," Grace added, not altogether in jest. The more she thought about it, the more she realized how much good it would do her and Sean to have a few days entirely to themselves, with no responsibilities, no worries...and no interruptions.

Sean chuckled. "Noted," he said. "We'll leave at the crack of dawn. Does that work?"

Grace rolled her eyes at him. "Ten o'clock as planned is fine, thank you." She turned to hug Gwyn around Julianne. "You're sure you're okay with handling our four for that long? You're not getting a lot of sleep as it is, and—"

"Alwyn and Steffan are here for another week. Between us and them, I think we have things covered." Gwyn hugged her back, then shooed her toward the front door as Gareth opened it. "Trying to get you two out of here is like herding cats, I swear. You have everything packed that you need, your reservation for the hotel tonight is confirmed, I'll take care of the dress, Gareth will return the tuxes tomorrow, and the kids are in good hands. No more excuses, all right? Get your tail ends out of here or I—"

"Excuse me," Gareth's deep voice cut across hers. "Can I help you?"

As one, Grace, Gwyn, and Sean craned their necks to see past him onto the night-shadowed porch. Grace blinked at what looked to be a pile of luggage, and then at the woman rising from the floorboards beside it. Unruly blonde curls framed a tired, wan face that seemed vaguely familiar, even though she would have sworn she'd never met the stranger. Beside her, Gwyn drew a quick, startled breath.

"*Abigail?*"

"Surprise," said the woman, giving a choked laugh as she spread her hands in a *well, here I am* gesture that encompassed the luggage. "I know you hadn't answered my letter yet, and I know I'm being presumptuous, but...."

Gwyn shifted Julianne to one arm as her sister's voice trailed off. She shook her head at Grace's silent offer to take the baby, her gaze remaining glued to the woman. A range of emotions flickering across her face: surprise, curiosity, reservation.

Any sign of welcome, however, remained noticeably lacking.

"What are you doing here?" she asked.

"I didn't want to crash the party. It was warm enough to sit out here on the porch, so I did."

Gwyn shook her head. "No. I meant what are you doing *here*. In Canada. And where are Olivia and Dominic?"

The woman's face crumpled like fragile tissue paper, and the sorrow behind her whispered response tore at Grace's very core. "They're gone, Gwyn." She wrapped her arms around herself, and for the first time, Grace noticed how thin she was beneath the summer-weight slacks and simple tank top she wore. She bit her bottom lip and lifted a bony shoulder in a half shrug. "They're gone, and I didn't know where else to go."

And with that, the woman began a slow slide toward the porch floor, as if she had used up the last of her energy and could no longer support her own body. Sean and Gareth both leapt through the doorway and caught her in mid collapse, then supported her between them into the house and the living room to the left of the entry hall. Grace touched Gwyn's arm.

"Gwyn? Are you all right?"

Gwyn roused herself to a wan smile and her gaze briefly met Grace's before flicking back to the living room. "I have no idea," she said.

Grace remembered what Gwyn had told her about Abigail's refusal to help when her ex had abandoned her, but try as she might to look at the woman through that lens, she couldn't get past her brokenness. She stared into the living room. The men had seated Abigail in an armchair, and Gareth crouched at her side while

Sean limped back toward the hallway. "She looks like she's in rough shape."

"I've never seen her like this," Gwyn admitted, her voice quiet. She raked her free hand through her hair. "Bloody hell, to quote my husband." Then she drew herself up as Sean reached them. "Well. None of this is your problem, and you have a honeymoon to attend, so off you go—and have a wonderful time. You've earned it."

Sean raised an eyebrow at Grace. She raised an eyebrow back. He nodded. She gave him a little smile. Not even a year together, and they'd already mastered the art of wordless communication.

"I'll make tea," she said, "and let Alwyn and Steffan know what's happening."

"I'll bring in Abigail's luggage," Sean replied.

"But—" Gwyn began.

Sean cut her off with a hug. "Family first," he said. "Right, Grace?"

For a fleeting moment, Grace remembered how she and Julianne had grown up, bounced from one relative's home to another, never wanted, forever an obligation. For so long, it had been just the two of them, clinging to one another for all they were worth. And then there had been Juli's children, and then the children but no Juli, and now...

Now she pictured the tumble of kids gathered in the kitchen for a bedtime snack under the close supervision of Alwyn and Steffan, who had crossed an ocean for them. She glanced into the living room, where Gareth remained on one knee beside a broken woman who needed her sister. Finally, she reached out to give her husband's hand a swift, grateful squeeze.

Family first, Sean had said.

"Always," she answered.

The End

Keep reading for a sneak peek at the next book

ABIGAIL ALWAYS

An Ever After Romance

Available Now

"You must have *something* I can do." Abigail Jamieson tried to keep the desperation out of her voice, but the way the woman across from her peered over her wire-rimmed glasses, she didn't think she'd succeeded. Through sheer force of will, she kept her hands linked loosely in her business-suited lap and didn't bolt for the door.

On the other side of the desk, Estelle Gagnon set aside the single sheet of paper that served as Abigail's scant resume. She leaned back in her chair and steepled her fingers, touching the index tips to her lips.

"Why childcare?" she asked finally, her English tinged by a slight French accent. "Why not something in an office?"

Abigail reached deep inside, past nerves left raw by answering this same question too many times over the last two weeks, and dug up the humility she needed to answer again. Nannies to Go was the last nanny agency on the list in the entire city of Ottawa, and she would not, could not, go home to her sister Gwyn's with no prospects yet again. Not after the conversation she'd overhead this morning.

"I know she needs our support, Gwyn," Gareth's voice floated through the door of his and Gwyn's bedroom as Abigail passed by in the hallway. *"But it's been three and a half months. And yes, she's helping out with the house, but you need your space back. We need our space back. At least let me put her up in an apartment while she figures out what she wants to do."*

"Are you going to be the one to tell her she's overstayed her welcome?" Gwyn retorted. *"She's my sister, Gareth, and her husband and daughter died. There is no way I'm turfing her out on her ear right now. She needs more time."*

"She's already been here almost three months. How much more time does she need? Another month? Three—"

"Mrs. Jamieson?"

The recruiter's voice jolted Abigail back to the present, and she pushed away the memory of her sister's disagreement with her husband. Over her. She crossed her ankles and tucked her feet under her chair, sitting up straighter. "I've been out of the workforce for a number of years," she said, with rehearsed calm. "And I don't have any office skills to speak of, beyond being able to use a computer."

"You don't have any childcare skills to speak of, either," Ms. Gagnon replied. "Most clients these days are looking for someone with a background in early childhood education at the very least. I'm afraid one semester of a psychology undergrad degree isn't quite the same, even if you did plan on going into child psychology. Without some kind of hands-on experience, there's nothing I can—"

"I had a daughter." The words spilled from Abby before she realized they'd even formed, surprising her as much as they obviously surprised Ms. Gagnon. The recruiter stared at her, eyebrows raised, waiting for more. Abby curled her hands into fists on her lap. It was the first time she'd told that to a stranger in more than a year. Or maybe it had been an eternity. "I had a daughter," she repeated, needing to say it again. Needing to hear it again. "She died."

Tears burned in the back of her eyes. Rapidly, she blinked them back as Ms. Gagnon stood up from her chair and crossed the office to a bookshelf under a window. She poured a glass of water from a pitcher there and returned to pass it to Abby. Then she leaned back against the desk. "When?" she asked, all trace of professionalism gone from her quiet voice.

"Just under a year ago," Abby said. "It was a car accident. She was eleven. She and my husband were both killed."

"I'm so sorry," said Ms. Gagnon. "Do you need a tissue?"

Abby gritted her teeth and shook her head. "Thank you, but I'm fine. Really."

"*Bon.*" Good. The recruiter went around the desk to retake her chair. She looked down at the resumé on the desk for a moment, then peered at Abby over her glasses again. "You're certain you want a job caring for children? It will not be too difficult for you?"

"I can manage," she said. "I've thought it through, and it really is the all I'm qualified for. To be honest, I've never even waitressed or worked in retail, and I would much rather work at something I know I can do."

Ms. Gagnon tapped a pen against the resumé. "There might be something, but..."

Abigail's hopes leapt. Oh, to go home and tell Gwyn she'd found something! "But?"

"You would have to live in, and there would be some housekeeping involved as well."

She clutched the glass tighter, needing an anchor in the sudden swirl of hope even as the irony made her want to laugh. Or cry. Or both. Oh, how William would love this, if he knew. All those fights over her desire for independence, for stimulation outside the home, and now look at her. Heading back into the kitchen to which he'd kept her tied for so many years. But...she'd get to move out of Gwyn and Gareth's house and actually stand—more or less—on her own two feet for the first time in a very, very long time.

Make that for the first time ever.

"I can definitely do that," she told Ms. Gagnon. "I was a stay-at-home..." She trailed off, the word *wife* stuck in her throat, and *mom* still too raw. She compromised with, "I stayed home for twelve years."

Something flashed in the recruiter's eyes—sympathy? pity?—but she moved the conversation along. "There are three girls: a five-year-old, a nine-year-old, and a thirteen-year-old. Their mother passed away just over a year ago—cancer—and their father is...struggling."

"Struggling?"

"He runs his own construction firm, and his hours can be irregular. He's trying his best, but honestly, he's losing ground every time I talk to him."

Abby frowned. "Every time you talk to him? How long has he been trying to find someone?"

Ms. Gagnon hesitated. Then she sighed. "I'm going to be honest with you, Mrs. Jamieson. This isn't an easy job. Frankly, I'm not even sure it's a doable job. If you take it, you'll be the twelfth woman to attempt it in the last nine months."

"Oh? What's the problem?"

"My client's hours. His unwillingness to back up the nannies on discipline issues. Discipline issues, period." Ms. Gagnon leaned back in her chair and sighed again. "My understanding is that the older girl resents having anyone tell her what to do. Part of the problem is the father's distraction, of course, and part of it may be the age of the nannies themselves. Most women who are coming out of early childhood education programs are young, and I'm not sure they have the air of authority that's needed here. You, on the other hand..."

Great. Now she was being offered a job because she was old? Abby tried not to grimace. She couldn't afford to be proud right now. Heck, she couldn't afford much of anything. She lifted her chin and took a deep breath.

"I'll take it," she said.

"Excellent. You can start as soon as your police check clears. I'll ask a friend to rush it."

Abigail stepped around her sister as Gwyn bounced a fussy Julianne against one shoulder, patting the baby's back with her free hand. She felt Gwyn's gaze on her, following her from bureau to closet to open suitcase on the bed. Studiously, she avoided meeting it.

"You're sure about this," Gwyn said for the fortieth time in the week since Abby had delivered her news. "I mean, a live-in *nanny*?"

Abby tried not to bristle at what sounded like criticism. Truth be told, if Gwyn *was* questioning her ability with children, she had good reason, because Abby had done her level best to avoid her nieces and nephew ever since her August arrival. At first, she'd told herself that it was because she couldn't handle being so close to what was obviously a happy family when she had lost so much. However, after three months, she'd begun to think it went deeper than that—into territory that included guilt and resentment and a whole lot of other baggage she didn't care to examine. That made it all the more important that she leave now, before the toxicity brewing deep in her gut found its way out and poisoned her relationship with her sister even more than it already had been for years. She took a pair of pants from a hanger and folded them into the suitcase.

"I'm sure," she replied, also for the fortieth time. "I need to move on with my life, Gwyn. I can't camp out here forever. Katie needs her room back." She glanced at the stuffed unicorns piled on a shelf and the *Anne of*

Green Gables series piled on the bedside table. *And I need not to be waking up every day in a room that could have been my own daughter's.*

"Katie is fine sharing with Maggie. This is about you." Gwyn wiped a trickle of drool from Julianne's chin, expertly following her daughter's twists and dodges and ignoring the squawks of protest. "I get that you want to move on, but raising someone else's children? What happened to that psychology degree you were studying for? Can't you do something with that instead?"

Abby closed her eyes. There was another thing she'd avoided since arriving here: any kind of conversation with Gwyn that touched on her life with William. For the same reasons she'd stopped writing to her sister about that life. Stopped confiding in her at all. Her cheeks grew hot, and she looked down at the floor. "I didn't finish," she answered, silently begging Gwyn not to pursue the subject.

"Oh," said her sister. Then, her voice hesitant, "Abby..."

"Don't." Abby shoved the last of her clothes, hangers and all, into the suitcase and slammed the lid down. She zipped it shut, then leaned on it, blinking back tears she didn't want to share. Didn't have the right to share, after she'd refused to be there when Gwyn had needed her—no matter what her reasons at the time. She straightened and turned, a tight smile pasted to her face. "I'm a big girl, Gwyn. I know what I'm doing."

"I'm not saying you don't. I'm just saying you don't have to do it. Stay. Please. Let us help."

Abby's resolve wavered in the face of the offer. Even after that conversation she'd overheard between Gwyn and Gareth last week, it would still be so much easier to remain here under their roof and their protection. So much safer. Except she'd lived her whole life sheltered from risk of any kind—first by her parents, and then by William—only to discover there was no such thing as safe. Life didn't care whether she actively participated in it or not; it happened regardless. With all of its pain and its grief and its loss...and its devastation. Again, Abby blinked back tears. Then she straightened her spine and shook her head. "Thank you, but no. I need to do this. I need to look after myself."

Gwyn gave a small, hesitant shrug. "All right," she said. "But you know you can come back, right? Anytime."

"I know."

"And, Abby...one day, when you're ready? Let's talk. Just the two of us. Please?"

Her eyes blurring and her throat refusing to allow words, Abby looked away from the sister she'd once adored. She didn't see how they would ever overcome the chasm that had grown between them, but she nodded anyway. Because, in a perfect world, she thought she'd like that.

If only a perfect world existed.

"Auntie Abby!" her nephew, Nicholas, hollered up the stairs. "Your taxi's here!"

Mitch Abrams pulled his head and shoulders out of the disaster that was the front hall closet and, sitting back on his heels, ran both hands over his close-cropped, tightly kinked hair. He locked his fingers behind his head. Then he regarded the solemn, five-year-old girl at eye level to him, stuffed plush rabbit under one arm and one Wonder Woman running shoe clutched in her other hand. One, because the other was missing.

"You're *sure* you put both of them in the closet after school yesterday?" he asked.

Kiana nodded, her lopsided puff ponytails bobbing.

"Maybe you can wear a different pair today."

Her gaze dropped to the floor, and she shook her head, shifting from foot to foot. Mitch's innards cringed at the telltale agitation. He unlinked his fingers and pushed himself to his feet. Eyes closed, he pinched the bridge of his nose and breathed deeply. He was already ten minutes late for a meeting with the crew on the new build, and if he triggered one of his daughter's infamous meltdowns, he might as well cancel it altogether.

"Dad! Daddy!" a voice hollered from the kitchen at the back of the house. "The pancakes are burning!"

The shriek of a smoke alarm confirmed the announcement. Face scrunched tight, Kiana dropped the running shoe and slapped her hands over her ears. Then she turned tail and bolted up the stairs, heading for the safety of her bedroom. Mitch groaned. Great. There went another hour of his morning.

"Daddy!" Louder this time. And shriller.

"Coming," he called back. He loped down the hallway to where his two other daughters, Brittany and Rachel, flapped tea towels at the smoke billowing across the room to the island where they sat. Thirteen-year-old Rachel delivered a withering look as he reached up to pull the smoke alarm from its housing inside the doorway and stuffed it in a drawer to muffle its noise.

"Again?" she asked.

"You could have flipped them," Mitch retorted. "Or at least turned the pan off." He switched off the stove and grabbed the skillet, pulling back with a hiss when he connected with red-hot metal. Scowling, he picked up a tea towel and wrapped it around the pan's handle, then carried it and its blackened contents over to the patio doors and tossed the entire works out into the snow. *Shit, shit, shit.* He slammed the glass door shut again, so hard that it bounced half out of its track, reminding him that he still hadn't repaired the thing. He scowled at the offending, lopsided glass panel. For six years, he'd promised Eve he'd fix it, and—

The doorbell rang.

"Oh, for—" Mitch scowled, then headed back down the hallway. Rachel trailed after him.

"You know that was our last frying pan, right?" she asked. "You threw the other one out last week."

Mitch ignored the accusatory tone. And the fact she was right. He kicked a path through the contents of the closet, still strewn across the front hall floor. How in hell had that much stuff fit in there in the first place?

"And what are we supposed to do about breakfast, now?" she continued. "Starve?"

"Madame Sonia says that breakfast is the most important meal of the day," nine-year-old Brittany offered, joining them in the chaos that had become a reflection of their lives. "She says—"

"Oh, stuff Madame Sonia," Rachel snapped. "She's not God, you know."

"Enough!" Mitch barked, his last nerve fraying as he reached for the door knob. "Brittany, Madame Sonia is right, but now is not the time. Rachel, apologize to your sister. Kiana! Kiana, *please* come downstairs. Daddy has to go to work, goddammit!" He wrenched open the door and bellowed, "What?"

He registered the smoky blue eyes first, the fur trim of a hood surrounding a pale face second, and the lazily drifting snowflakes third. He didn't recognize the first two, but he knew without a doubt that the last observation had just killed all hope of making it into work that day. There was no army on the planet that could get Kiana into winter boots or a snowsuit without a week of advance warning, and with him not having so much as checked the forecast for the last several days, that opportunity had passed him by.

"Shit," he said, staring morosely out at the four inches of white fluff already piled up on the lawn. He recalled an image of the blackened frying pan landing in more of the stuff just moments before—he'd just been too distracted to pay attention. His gaze went back to the uninvited guest on his doorstep, traveling from head to toe. A woman, wearing a bright red jacket, pleated slacks, and the kind of furry boots Rachel had whined about for the last three Christmases and he had deemed ridiculous. He looked up again. A tiny frown had appeared between the smoky blue eyes.

"Mr. Abrams?"

He scowled. How in heck was he going to talk Kiana into anything halfway suitable for going to school? "Who wants to know?"

A white-mittened hand extended. "I'm Abigail Jamieson."

He stared at the hand.

"From the agency?" she prompted.

He stared at her.

"The nanny agency. Nannies to Go? I left you a voicemail message on Friday telling you I'd be here at 8:oo this morning."

"Daddy? Who's that?" Brittany wedged herself between Mitch's hip and the doorframe.

Smoky Eyes smiled down at her and again held out the hand Mitch had refused to shake. "My name is Abigail," she said. "But you can call me Abby. And I'm guessing you must be Brittany."

Brittany eyed the offered mitten for a second, then she accepted it and gave it a hearty pump. "Pleased to meet you," she said. "Are you really our new nanny?"

"I am," the woman said.

"No. She's not," Mitch overrode her words. He ran a hand over his chinstrap beard. The scrape of stubble against his palm outside the normal confines reminded him he had yet to tidy it this morning. Or shower. He held back the choice epithets growling through his brain. Maybe he should just give up and see if he could talk Derek into handling the meeting for him. Hell, maybe he should just give up on the whole blasted—

He cut the thought short and waved a hand in half-hearted apology. "Look, I'm sorry, but I haven't checked my voicemail all week, I know nothing about a new nanny, and I don't have time to interview anyone right now. Tell the agency to call me again next week, and we'll set something up."

His hand on Brittany's shoulder, he stepped back and started to close the door.

"Wait!" The white mitten shot through the opening and fastened around the edge. "I'm not here for an interview. I'm here to work!"

Mitch pulled the door open a fraction again and peered around it. For the first time, he noticed the pile of luggage on the snow-covered sidewalk behind her. One large roll-along suitcase, one medium-sized one, and an overnight bag. He raised an eyebrow. Met the blue gaze. Raised the other eyebrow. "Work?" he echoed. "As in *move in?*"

The fur-framed face went even paler as the

woman's expression wobbled, then tightened. Her voice dropped to barely a whisper. "I thought—I was told— Estelle said—"

"Estelle?"

"Ms. Gagnon. At Nannies to Go." The woman bit her bottom lip. "She said it was a live-in position."

"Not without a freaking interview, it isn't." Mitch looked her up and down again. "Do you really think I'd let someone move in with my children without meeting them first? Seeing their references? What the hel—heck kind of a parent would that make me?"

The blue gaze traveled past him to the shambles that was his front hall, and Mitch was pretty certain the words "a desperate one" hovered on her lips. He bristled, but to her credit, she kept the comment to herself as she squared her shoulders and nodded.

"Of course. I should have—I'm sorry. I'll let Est— Ms. Gagnon know. We can do an interview whenever you're ready." She waved her mitten at the luggage. "I'll need a cab, if you wouldn't mind calling one for me?"

His gaze went to the driveway, empty of any vehicle but his own pickup. Great. Now he was turning her away in the snow and cold? His conscience twinged, but sheer practicality overruled it. He was in no way prepared to take in a new nanny without any kind of warning, he knew nothing about this particular wannabe, he was growing later by the second for that meeting, and he still had three girls to crowbar and/or cajole out of the house. He firmed his jaw. "Of course," he said. "And we'll set up something for later this week. Maybe Thursday evening?" Then, because he'd been rather shorter with her than was needed, he added, "I'm sorry for the mix-up."

Horror filled him as the blue eyes turned shiny. Oh hell, no. She wasn't going to cry, was she? Could this morning possibly get any worse? As he debated closing the door on her—admittedly not his most stellar moment as a human being—a car horn tooted curbside and a cheery voice called out, "Morning, Mitch! The girls ready to go?"

Rachel shoved him aside and waved to her best friend's mother, a woman as comfortable with her generous curves as she was with her status as a divorcée.

"We'll be there in a minute, Jessica!" she called. Then, ignoring the woman standing on the porch, she crossed her arms and scowled up at Mitch. "You forgot that you asked Mandy's mom to pick us up for school starting this week, didn't you?"

"I—"

"And we still haven't had breakfast. What are we supposed to do, starve?"

Mitch bit back the uncharitable *yes* that hovered and instead said, "Just get ready. I'll get some granola bars from the kitchen." He turned back to the open door. "Ms. Jamieson, was it? I'm sorry, but I really ha—" He stopped mid-sentence as Jessica Perkins danced up onto the porch to join the wannabe nanny. Hell.

"Oh dear." She pulled a face as her gaze went to the hallway behind him. "Rough morning? You really should take me up on my offer to get you guys organized, Mitch, my friend. A couple of weeks and you won't even recognize the place."

The air wheezed from Mitch. Oh, he'd seen Jessica's house, all right. The woman had invited the girls to go swimming in her pool in August, and then insisted on giving him the grand tour while wearing the skimpiest bikini he'd ever tried not to lay eyes on. He all but broke out in a cold sweat at the memory of how many times he'd had to extricate himself from various corners of that place. He didn't think the woman had any serious designs on him, but she had made it abundantly clear that she thought two lonely people could—and should—find solace in one another's company. But she was right—her corners had been organized. He just had no intention of putting himself in a similar situation again.

"Thanks, Jessica, but—"

"Oh, pooh," Jessica waved away the objection. "You know it's no trouble. I'm happy to help. Why don't Mandy and I come over tomorrow after school? The girls can hang out, and I can get a start. We'll order pizza for dinner. It will be fun!" Without waiting for a response, she turned to the other woman. "I'm so sorry. How rude of me not to introduce myself. I'm Jessica Perkins, a family friend."

"Abigail Jamieson," Smoky Eyes murmured.

Was it Mitch's imagination, or was she trying not to laugh?

"I see," Jessica said, when no further information was offered. She nodded at the luggage pile she'd skirted on her way up the sidewalk. "And you're here...for a visit?"

"I'm—"

"She's moving in with us!" Brittany poked her head past Mitch, her voice muffled by the scarf she'd wound around her face. "She's our new nanny."

"Oh?" Jessica looked over her shoulder at Mitch. "Rachel didn't mention you'd found someone new."

Mitch opened his mouth to explain, then closed it as an image of Jessica Perkins organizing his house popped into his head. Another one followed of her wearing a bikini while doing so.

On the porch, Abigail Jamieson steadfastly refused to meet his gaze.

Abigail Jamieson, his unexpected—and unsuspecting—lifeline.

"It was a last-minute thing," he heard himself reply.

"I see." Jessica's narrow gaze traveled between Mitch and Abigail Jamieson, who stared down at a hole she'd made in the snow with the toe of her furry boot. Then Jessica's expression cleared, becoming cheerful again and leaving Mitch wondering what she saw.

"Well then," she said, "Welcome, Abigail Jamieson. I'll leave you to get settled in, but make sure Mitch leaves you my number in case you need anything while he's at work. I'm happy to help if I can. Come on, girls, we're running late."

With a cheery wave, she trotted back down the driveway to the car she'd left idling, the snow swallowing the sound of her door closing. A second later, Rachel shoved past him, Brittany on her heels.

"Bye, Daddy!" Brittany sang over her shoulder. "Bye, Abby! See you after school!"

"Wait," Mitch called after them. "Granola bars!"

Rachel waved a handful of wrapped bars aloft as she trudged across the lawn. She didn't deign to look back. Seconds later, Jessica's car disappeared down the road, and silence fell over the yard, as thick and muffled as the flakes descending now in earnest. On the porch, Abigail Jamieson stamped her ridiculous boots and wrapped her arms around herself.

Mitch sighed. Now that he'd made it past the knee-jerk reaction to her arrival, maybe giving her a try wouldn't be such a bad idea. Because the look she'd given his hallway was right. He was desperate. And he'd run through so many nannies in the last year that he'd been blacklisted by just about every agency in town. And Estelle Gagnon had assured him that every nanny she sent out had already passed a police check. And if he didn't find help soon, a lot more than the house was going to go south in his life. And—

He held the door wide. "I assume you have references?" he asked.

Like all romance writers, Linda Poitevin is a firm believer in happy-ever-afters, but she also knows how hard you have to work at relationships sometimes. She tries to reflect that in stories about people who live, laugh, cry, and love just as hard as they can in this crazy life we all share—people who are as real to her as she hopes they'll be to you.

Linda lives outside Ottawa, Canada's capital, where (in her other-than-writing life) she is a wife, mom, friend, avid gardener, walker of a giant dog, and keeper of many (many!) pets. She also writes dark urban fantasy under the name of Lydia M. Hawke.

You can find Linda on her website at LindaPoitevin.com (sign up for her newsletter there to get book updates!) or shoot her an email (she loves to hear from readers!) at info@LindaPoitevin.com.

OTHER BOOKS BY LINDA POITEVIN

Gwynneth Ever After

Forever After

Forever Grace

Abigail Always

Shadow of Doubt

Writing as Lydia M. Hawke

Sins of the Angels

Sins of the Son

Sins of the Lost

Sins of the Warrior

www.ingramcontent.com/pod-product-compliance
Lightning Source LLC
Chambersburg PA
CBHW030817200726
48288CB00004B/1266